The Isle of Avalon

The Talisman - Book VII

The
Isle of
Avalon

Michael Harling

ISBN: 979-8-9907389-7-3

Published in the US and UK in 2024
by Lindenwald Press

iv

Lindenwald **LP** Press

To Mitch and Charlie
Without whom there would be no story.

Also by Michael Harling

The Postcards Trilogy
Postcards From Across the Pond
More Postcards From Across the Pond
Postcards From Ireland

The Talisman Series
The Magic Cloak
The Roman Villa
The Sacred Tor
The Bard of Tilbury
The Crystal Palace
The White Feather

Finding Rachel Davenport

Chapter 1
Tuesday, 16 June 2019

Mitch

The feather changed everything.

If I lived a normal life, I'd have been enjoying myself that summer, reading, playing Flight Simulator on my computer, swimming, or throwing a ball around with my brother Charlie. But I didn't live a normal life, and neither did Charlie, which was why we found ourselves getting a lecture from Dad, at eight o'clock on a Tuesday morning, when he should have been at work.

"You're not getting them," Dad said. He didn't look at us as he spoke. Instead, he kept his eyes on the floor, pacing between us and the dining table, where two swords lay next to an upturned box and a pile of packing material.

Charlie pointed at the swords. "Dad, they're wooden."

"That's not the point," he said, still studying the floor.

I didn't say anything. I just looked at the swords, and then at Mom, who hovered near the edge of the argument. She had her arms folded across her chest and a stormy look on her face. The look wasn't meant for us, however, it was Dad she was glaring at. Dad didn't look at her, or us, or the swords. He just kept staring at the floorboards, as if wishing they would open up and swallow him. "I don't care what they're made out of," he said, "this has got to stop."

I agreed with him; it was senseless. Every summer we got a gift from Granddad, and every summer a bigger argument erupted. Then Mom started trying to get the gifts before we could. Fortunately, I had figured out that the gifts always arrived with the full moon, and that had given us an advantage for a while because we could get to the mailbox before her. But Mom figured that out too, and this year, she'd gone to the Post Office to get the gifts before they even sent it out with the mailman, and she had returned triumphant.

She had grabbed Dad as he was on his way to work and shouted for us to appear before her. She'd opened the box, put the crude, wooden swords on the dining table, and ordered Dad to tell us we couldn't have them. Dad looked like he'd rather be anywhere else, and Charlie and I were just tired of the whole thing.

The idea that granddad was still sending gifts was, itself, ridiculous. It was as if he believed we were still seven, instead of eighteen, and still enjoyed engaging in fantasy adventures.

"You can't take my stuff, Dad," Charlie said, "it's, like, illegal—"

At last, Dad looked up. He pointed a finger at Charlie's face. "As long as you live in this house …"

I tuned him out. If we'd lived normal lives, there would be no argument. Mom would just give us the gifts. And if she didn't want to, we could simply walk away. That's what I felt like doing now, and it's what I would have done, if it hadn't been for the feather.

Upstairs, in my bedroom, hidden between the pages of a book, was a feather, given to me by Annie McAllister, over one hundred years ago. It came back with us from the adventure we'd had last summer, the only thing—aside from us, the cloak, and Granddad's gifts—that had ever travelled with us. In other years, memories of our travels faded with time, until we'd wonder if they had simply been vivid dreams. But the feather kept them sharp. Every time I held it, memories of Annie welled inside me, fresh and clear as the morning we'd met. I felt her hand in mine, the taste of her kiss, the terror of losing her, the relief in her embrace, and the ache of parting.

That rush of emotion proved the adventures weren't simply made-up fantasies; they were real, as true and certain as her love for me, and mine for her. And it meant the swords were more important than Dad or Mom, understood. And it meant we couldn't walk away.

I looked at Charlie. Dad had finished his lecture and resumed his study of the floor. He paced in front of us, then back towards Mom. When he was as far from us as he was going to get, with his back to the dining table, I nodded at Charlie, and Charlie nodded back. We each drew a breath, then sprang forward, and grabbed the swords.

Dad spun around. "Hey!"

We raced to the stairs, scaling them two at a time with Dad behind us bellowing like an angry bull. That didn't bother me as much as Mom, who was behind him, screaming, not in anger, but with raw panic.

I cleared the top step with Charlie beside me and Dad not far behind. We bounded into my bedroom, slammed the door, and jammed the chair under the doorknob just as Dad hit it. The door boomed and bowed, and the chair creaked, but it held, for now. From the other side, Dad shouted, Mom pleaded and cried, and then the door boomed again.

I felt the blood drain from my face. Charlie tugged on my arm. "C'mon, we don't have much time. And whatever is waiting for us won't be as bad as what will happen if Dad breaks the door down before we get away."

We ran to my bed, where the cloak was already laid out. We knelt on the mattress, facing each other, chest to chest, with the swords between us, and flung the cloak over our heads.

"Like we practiced," I shouted into Charlie's face. "Ten times. Go!"

We breathed, fast and deep, counting as we did.

"1, 2, 3, 4 ..."

The door boomed. The chair creaked.

"5, 6, 7, 8 ..."

Another boom, another shout, and the sound of wood cracking.

"9, 10, squeeze."

We wrapped our arms around each other, squeezing hard. I held my breath as Charlie's arms pressed against my back and the swords dug so painfully into my chest I wanted to cry out. But I held on, and kept my arms locked around Charlie, squeezing as hard as I could.

Another boom. The chair snapped. The door

slammed open. Footsteps, loud and heavy rushed in, accompanied by shouts and screams. I waited for the hands that would snatch the cloak off us and shake us until our teeth rattled. Then Charlie went slack, and my head spun and, even though my eyes were closed, I saw black blossoms exploding, bleeding into one another, covering me in darkness.

And then I was falling.

Chapter 2
September 537 AD

Charlie

Before I even opened my eyes, I knew the plan had worked. Mainly, I wasn't being dragged downstairs with Dad shouting and Mom screeching, but also, I was lying on a bed of spiky leaves instead of a mattress, and there was no sound except the distant twitter of birds and the gentle tap of rain. I breathed in, smelling the dank air and feeling the weight of the sword on my chest.

We had practiced all week, using those rare times when both Mom and Dad were out. We practiced running up the stairs from every location in the house. We practiced shutting and barring the door with the chair and pulling the cloak over ourselves. And we also practiced the trick John had shown us when we travelled to the Crystal Palace with him in 1851. He had incapacitated a man by squeezing him until he passed out and had shown us how it was done. We had to refine the technique and try it, time and again, on each other until we finally got it right. Then we practiced doing it on each other at the same time. That proved tricky, as it required both of us to pass out simultaneously and remain under the cloak when we fell. It also gave us headaches.

We knew, however, that it might be necessary, and our time in Harold's army had taught us that it is better to be over prepared than to be caught unprepared, so we kept practicing, and I'm glad we did.

On the day of the full moon, Mom intercepted the package at the Post Office, just like we figured she would. What we hadn't counted on was her keeping Dad home. We didn't know she had been working on him for weeks, wearing him down and getting him on her side. We also didn't know that the gifts would be swords. All we knew was, whatever Granddad sent us, she would try to keep it from us. And that could not be allowed to happen. Like Mitch, I now had the knowledge that what we were doing was real. And while that scared me to death, it also meant we were supposed to go, no matter what the gift was, and no matter where the cloak sent us. If I hadn't known, I'd have just walked away.

Mitch's knowledge came from the feather his girlfriend gave him; mine from a photograph taken in 1916: a photograph of us, me and Mitch, at the bombed-out building where we had appeared. I suppose another sort of person—a sane one, for instance—might think, "Hey, if this is real, I'm for sure *not* going," but to us, it made it seem like we had no choice. Were we the smart ones, or the dumb ones, or the sane ones? It didn't bear thinking about, because we were already there.

I pushed the cloak off and sat up. The sword clanked to the ground next to me. It was real now, long and broad, and in a leather scabbard trimmed with metal. Beside me, Mitch groaned and held his head. "Either we passed out, or dad just whacked me."

"You're safe," I said, "for now, anyway."

Mitch sat up, hefting his sword in both hands. "This is heavy, and there's no belt with it. How are we supposed to carry them?"

I stood, pulling the cloak up with me. The branches of the trees were low enough that the spiny leaves pricked my head, and I had to stoop to avoid getting stuck. Glossy green foliage surrounded us, locking us in an emerald room with the Middle Ages version of barbed wire. At least I assumed it was the Middle Ages. It had that feel; a sense of emptiness, a world waiting to be filled. I began folding the cloak into a bundle, as Ellen had shown me when we visited in 1588, and looked down at Mitch. "When do you think this is?"

Mitch looked around at the leaves surrounding us. "That's holly."

I continued folding the cloak. "And?"

Mitch climbed to his feet, stooping to avoid the leaves, and turned slowly around. "This looks familiar. Remember our first adventure? We started out in a forest, inside a ring of holly bushes."

I looked up and studied a leaf. "Yeah, it's holly, but these aren't bushes."

"Maybe it's a few years later."

I finished disguising the cloak. It now looked like a typical bundle, something a traveller would carry. I tested it to be sure I could hold it easily with one hand. I would need the other to carry my sword. I looked at the wall of holly and brambles fencing us in.

"There's only one way to find out."

I put the cloak down and we both picked up our swords. Last time, getting out of the holly-ring had been difficult and painful; this time, we just hacked a hole and ducked through it into the forest.

Out from under the holly, it was brighter, but the soft rain that couldn't penetrate the tangle of holly leaves now dripped through to the forest floor, just enough to be annoying. I looked around. Nothing seemed familiar.

"Which way?" Mitch asked.

I peered through the forest. "There's no road, no path, just like when we were first here."

"And which way did we go then?"

"I can't remember, and there's not even any sun to help us."

Mitch looked up through the trees. "It's cloudy, drizzling, and cool. It could be any month of the year, and any time of the day."

I took a few tentative steps, struggling to remember the lay of the land. Holly bushes aside, there was really no reason to think we had arrived in the same spot as we had on our first visit, other than the fact that this was the spot we had arrived at in every subsequent adventure. So, I made that assumption, and took another good look around. "The land seems to drop in this direction. As I recall, there's a stream somewhere around here. If we keep to the downslope, we're sure to hit it sooner or later."

Mitch agreed that was as good a plan as any, so we hacked our way through the undergrowth, more as a way to mark our path so we could return, than out of necessity. Within the forest, it was dark, which kept the undergrowth thin and the travel easy. Soon, however, the trees became sparse, and the brush thickened, and forward movement became a challenge.

We were slowed to the point where I had to put the cloak down and swing my sword with both hands. Mitch stood next to me, swinging his own sword. When he chopped a branch from a stunted tree he stopped and put a hand on my shoulder. "Look at this."

I left off hacking at the wall of brush in front of me. "What?"

"This is an apple tree. An old, uncultivated apple tree."

I looked at the fallen branch, then at the tree, and then at a similar tree not far from it, and another one beyond that. "When we were in Roman times, this was an apple orchard."

Mitch pointed to a distant hump in the ground. "That looks like the remains of a wall."

We groped our way to it. It was a wall, or the moss and weed-covered base of one, leading in the direction we wanted to go. The line of rocks paved a relatively easy path through the heavy growth, and we followed it to a corner, where the wall continued next to a faint line of packed earth, which we took to be the ghost of the old farm road. We hacked our way along that and soon the growth thinned, and an open area came into view. I jogged forward and clambered onto a long line of flat stones. "It's the Roman road. Horsham is this way."

We walked quickly, and with growing confidence.

Soon, we crossed the stone bridge, and the area began to look familiar.

"In that thicket," Mitch said, pointing with his sword, "that's where Pendragon told us the giants lived. He must have been referring to the ruins of Fabianus's farm."

I peered through the tangle of brush, at the humps in the ground and the few, remaining stone columns, trying to remember how they used to look some two-hundred and fifty years earlier. "Yes," I said, "it all makes sense now."

"Given the way people are living now, it's no wonder they thought they were giants."

I nodded in agreement, then got a sudden, unpleasant feeling. "Speaking of people, where are they?"

Chapter 3

Mitch

We stopped and looked up the road, and down the road. There was no one in sight.

"Maybe it's a slow day," Charlie said.

I tried to convince myself that was it. After all, we hadn't seen Horsham like this in a long time, so it could be that this was normal. Each adventure had brought us closer to the modern era, so we were getting used to seeing more people. But now, the buildings were gone, there were no cars, no paved roads, no houses, or mills, or shops. And no people.

We continued towards the town, or where the town used to be. If we were in the era I suspected we were in, Horsham would be a small village instead of a town, little more than a clearing in the forest.

This was confirmed when, a short time later, the brush gave way to a few small fields, and unpleasant odours mingled with the fresh air. In the distance, a scattering of cottages with a rutted lane running between them came into view and, on the near edge of the village, was the Green Dragon public house, now a stone and wood building with a thatched roof and a few rough benches in the muddy yard. Its door was barred, however, and its windows dark. The first time we had seen it, there had been men sitting on the benches, drinking, and listening to a knight telling tales of bravery in an attempt to shame them into helping him slay a dragon. But now, there was simply silence, in the pub, and in the village.

"I don't like this," Charlie said, staring down the empty street. "It looks like it's been deserted."

I sniffed the air and wrinkled my nose. "It's not deserted. The mud is fresh, and it stinks. That means there are people, and animals, here."

"Then where are they?"

I couldn't think of any answer I wanted to speak out loud. They might have all died of the plague or been frightened off (or killed) in an attack. What I did say was, "The dragons might have returned."

Charlie merely grimaced. We walked slowly to the edge of the village, peering around us, speaking in whispers, as if we had entered someone's house uninvited.

"Nothing," Charlie said. "Not a soul, not a sound."

I looked at the dark, silent houses, their doors and windows barred.

"This feels strange. But the town, I mean the village, it does look familiar. It's like it was when we first visited, I get the feeling this isn't too long after we left. It sorta looks the same, but older, and sadder."

"And emptier," Charlie said.

We turned away and started down the narrow track that led to the River Arun, and the path that would take us to Pendragon's house. The way was rutted by wagon wheels and pocked with fresh hoof prints of cows and horses, but we saw no one. Aside from the rain that continued to drip from the grey sky, everything remained still, and silent.

Then the hair on the back of my neck stood up, and I felt as if a dozen pairs of eyes were fixed on me. I stopped, turned slowly, and looked towards the Green Dragon.

The door was open now, and several faces peered out. Standing in front of them was a knight wearing a breast plate and chain mail, his gloved fists resting on his hips, his feet planted wide in the mud. He held my gaze and placed one hand on the hilt of the sword hanging from his leather belt. Behind him, the other men ducked back inside the pub. On his breast plate, visible even from that distance, was the emblem of a black dragon.

I turned away, pretending not to be startled, even as a tingle ran down my spine and my stomach knotted. I quickened my pace and caught up with Charlie. "I know where the people are," I said. "They're hiding."

"From what?"

"Us, I think."

Chapter 4

Charlie

I resisted the urge to look back and kept walking as if nothing was wrong. Ahead of us, we saw the stone bridge that spanned the River Arun. It was just as we remembered, and to the left was the path that ran along the river to Pendragon's.

"This is getting spooky," I said, as we left the track and started down the path. "Why is everyone inside?"

Mitch shrugged. "I don't know, but it's making me nervous."

I felt a tightening in my chest. "Me too," I said, coming to a halt. "I vote we go back."

Mitch stopped and turned to face me. I could tell he felt the same. "That would be the smart thing to do," he said, "but it doesn't feel like the right thing." He took a deep breath and looked around at the seemingly peaceful countryside. "Besides, we're in no more danger now than we were on any other adventure." He smiled weakly, but it didn't reassure me.

"That's not saying much," I said, "we were almost killed last time."

He said nothing. He merely nodded and glanced over his shoulder in the direction of Pendragon's house, the place where the adventures always begin. We both knew, if we kept going, it would soon be too late to turn back, if it wasn't already. "Do you really want to abandon this and go back home?"

"Yes," I said, "but …"

Mitch looked at me, his brow furrowed. "But what?"

I shrugged. "In every adventure, we do something dangerous, and whatever we end up doing here will be just as dangerous. So, nothing has changed except now we know it's real, and that scares me."

Mitch looked at the ground. "If it helps, I'm scared too. But, just like all the other times, I know we'll get home eventually."

Then the feeling I had been trying to tease out of the confusion became clear. "That's just it, this one isn't like all the other times. This one feels different." I swung the sword in an arc, pointing to the trees, the river, the empty path. "This is where it all began, here, in this time. This is where we met Pendragon, Aisley and Garberend. And it feels like this is where it's going to end. Like we've come full circle, like we're here to wrap things up." I dropped my arm to my side and looked at Mitch. "It feels like, if we don't leave now, we're never going to get back."

Mitch looked at the ground and shuffled his feet. "Every adventure feels like that but, somehow, we always managed to survive, and we will this time too."

"But this time, we know," I said. "This isn't a fantasy, this isn't a game, this isn't some elaborate dream." I pointed with the tip of my sword again. "This is real."

Mitch nodded. "So make sure it doesn't cloud your judgment. More than ever, we're going to need our wits about us. If you decide to come, that is."

I sighed. Did I really have a choice? The fact that it was real meant that what we did mattered. Going back wasn't an option, even though I felt like going forward meant certain death. "Yes, I'm coming."

Mitch smiled. "Then let's go."

He turned and walked on and, after a second or two, I followed.

Soon, the stone cottage, its yard now cluttered and overrun with weeds, came into sight. It was the same farm we had seen on our first adventure, which had been six years ago for us. I wondered how many years had passed here.

We stepped through a gap in the stone fence where a gate used to be, but no dogs barked, no chickens scattered, and no one came out to greet us. We walked forward slowly. The house remained silent, its windows barred and the door, which was little more than a few rough boards held together with leather straps, hung askew. Then the door creaked open, and an old woman lurched out.

Her grey hair was tied up, partly covered by a torn scarf, and she wore a shapeless dress that reached nearly to her bare feet. We froze, stunned and confused. She shuffled towards us and fell to her knees. We dropped our swords and the cloak and grabbed her by her arms to keep her from falling in the dirt.

Blood dripped from her nose and oozed from the bruises in her cheeks. Her eyes were clear and alert, however, and she looked at us with recognition.

"Mitch, Charlie," she said, in a voice I could scarcely hear.

"Aisley?" I asked.

She nodded and drew a ragged breath to speak again. We leaned close and her voice came as a low rasp.

"Run."

Chapter 5

Mitch

The silence was shattered as a half dozen men, dressed in light armour and chainmail, rushed from the house, drawing their swords, and yelling as they bounded towards us.

"Let's go," Charlie shouted.

We tried to pull Aisley to her feet, but she shook her head. "Leave me. Go. Run."

Shouts came from behind us. I turned and saw another half-dozen men swooping into the yard, cutting off our escape. I dived for my sword, but a heavy boot stepped on it and another kicked me from behind, sending me sprawling in the dirt.

"Grab them," someone shouted. "And bring the woman."

I rolled onto my back and found myself facing four drawn swords. Charlie and Aisley were surrounded by four other men, and others were taking our swords, and the cloak, into the house.

Someone yanked me to my feet, twisted my arms behind my back, and shoved me towards the house. My eyes watered from the pain, and shouts echoed in my ears as I stumbled forward. The door, I noticed as we passed through, was not ajar as I had thought, but splintered, and hanging from a single hinge. Inside the dim room, chairs, stools, and a small table were scattered over the floor. Shelves hung askew on the walls, and clay jars lay smashed on the floor, their contents oozing over the reeds that covered the bare earth. A low fire smouldered in the central fire pit, filling the room with a smoky haze that stung my eyes and burned my throat.

Rough hands propelled me further into the gloom. Then I saw Charlie beside me, coughing and struggling against his captor. Beyond the confusion, at the edge of the room, two men shoved Aisley into a chair. One of the men stood behind her, his brawny hands gripping her shoulders. The other, the shorter and fatter of the two, with a walrus moustache on his upper lip, a sword on his belt and a dagger in his hand, stood in front.

We stumbled forward, towards a table at the back of the room. It was long and thick and supported by sturdy legs and, even through the haze, I recognized it as the table we had sat around with Pendragon and his family, the one that had originally been the door when the house was a Roman slave cottage, the same table we had sat around last year—or a hundred years ago, or fifteen hundred years in the future (it was all a little confusing)—for a meal with Annie and her aunt Maggie.

I thought they meant to shove us under it, but we were jerked to a halt, and a knight laid our cloak on the tabletop. Another brought our swords and dropped them onto the hard wood. They landed with a loud clank that cut through the noise and confusion and, suddenly, everything went silent.

Behind the table, the darkness stirred. Someone was sitting there.

"Well, well, this is quite a surprise."

The man leaned forward. He nodded at our captors, and they released my arms, sending tingles of pain down my shoulders. Behind me, swords returned to their scabbards. The man in front of Aisley sheathed his dagger, but the other kept her firmly pressed into the chair. One of the men lit an oil lamp on the table. Others opened the shutters and, as light slowly filtered through the smoke, the man became visible. He was broad-shouldered and dressed in armour, with a black dragon adorning his breastplate. His face was hard and scarred and framed by black hair that hung to his shoulders.

He rose from his seat and stood with his hands on the table, leaning forward, peering at us. Then he lifted one of our swords, pulled it partway out of the scabbard, and appraised it. "And what have we here? A battle sword?" He slid it back into the scabbard and lifted the cloak. As it unfurled, a grin spread across his face. He dropped it and leaned forward to peer at us again, then he sat down.

"It is you," he said, leaning back in his chair, stroking his scruffy beard. It wasn't a chair that belonged to the house. Compared to the rough seats scattered around the room, it looked like a throne. It was high-backed, ornately carved, and had cushioned arms. It must have been looted from one of the other houses and brought here to add to his comfort and ability to intimidate. "The meddling children have returned at last, but ..." He put his elbows on the table and rested his chin in his hands. "Twenty summers have passed since those days, and you have aged little. What sorcery is this? Are you one of the immortals?"

I studied the man's face. In the flickering lamplight, his features were distorted by shadow, yet the set of his jaw and narrowness of his eyes looked familiar. I was just about to say the name when an elbow slammed into my side. "Speak when Lord Fergus asks you a question."

I held my side, gasping for breath. It was Fergus, the knight who had taken us captive. The friend of Mordred, King Arthur's son. Both had double-crossed us, and each other, in their bid to keep our cloak, and the Talisman, for themselves, until we had finally won it from them in a jousting match. Whatever he was involved in, it couldn't be good, and he wasn't going to look favourably on us.

"No," I said. "We are not immortal. We are travellers."

"Hmm," Fergus said, "and from what land do you travel?"

I looked at Charlie and shrugged. "Wynantskill."

"Liars!" Fergus said, springing from his seat. Charlie and I jumped as he leaned across the table, his eyes shining in the flickering light. "When you ran away, we searched the known world for this kingdom of Wynantskill, and it does not exist, and you were nowhere to be found."

"We didn't run," Charlie said. "Our work was finished. We returned to our home."

"And where was that?"

Charlie and I looked at each other, sighed, and

22

said, "Wynantskill."

We braced ourselves for another tantrum, but Fergus just sat and resumed his beard stroking. "We heard rumours that you would one day return, but you never did. We assumed your cowardice kept you hidden, yet here you are, as contrary as ever, and at the most auspicious of times." He stopped stroking and looked towards the ceiling, which was really the underside of the thatched roof, pondering. Then he looked at us. "This cannot be coincidence."

He stood again, still staring at us, his fingers absently running over the fabric of our cloak. "I am on a quest to find your friend, Pendragon, and time is of the essence. Your return tells me God is on our side. You are here for a reason: to meet Pendragon, and you will tell me where he is."

"We don't know where he is," I said. "We came here to *look* for Pendragon."

"Someone in this god-forsaken village is hiding him, and you will tell me who that person is."

"That's why no one is outside," Charlie said. "You're holding the whole town prisoner."

Fergus slammed his hand on the table. "I am conducting an investigation," he shouted. "They are not cooperating, but you will. Unlike them, I am certain you have the information. Now tell me, where is he?"

"We don't know," I said.

"He's your friend, you came to meet him. How can you not know where he is?"

"Maybe he doesn't want to be found," Charlie said.

Fergus smirked and gestured towards Aisley. "That's what the woman says. Is that the best you can do, hide behind the lies of a weak woman?"

I looked around the room. It was filled with armed men, and Aisley, bloodied and bruised, in the chair, with guards on either side of her.

"A weak woman? It took more than a dozen of your men to subdue her. How many did it take to hold her until you felt safe enough to punch her in the face?"

Fergus sat, saying nothing. At length, he spoke, his voice tight. "You will regret your insolence." He looked at Aisley. "This woman would rather die than reveal the whereabouts of her son, but I don't believe you will."

"Threatening to kill us won't do you any good," Charlie said. "We don't know."

"A convenient lie," Fergus said, "but I do believe you would also prefer death over betrayal. But it would not be a betrayal. We need Pendragon to perform a valuable service for the King. That is why I must find him. I am here to bestow an honour upon him."

I couldn't believe he'd need to interrogate the town and torture Aisley if he was really here to give Pendragon a medal. But it didn't really matter, because …

"We don't know where he is," I said, again.

Fergus grinned in a way that left me cold. "You do, and you will tell me. I don't doubt you'd welcome an honourable death—"

"Actually," Charlie said "we'd like to avoid that if

we could—"

"Silence." Fergus leaned over the table again, his nose a sword-length from mine. All his men had backed away, leaving Fergus and us, and Aisley and her two minders, at the end of the room with a semicircle of men watching from beyond the sputtering fire. His grin widened, showing yellow teeth. "Your own deaths would be easy for you to take, but you would not want to cause the death of another. Tell me where Pendragon is, or the woman dies."

The man behind Aisley gripped her arms and pinned her tightly against the back of the chair, the other drew his dagger.

"But we don't know," Charlie said, pleading, "we can't know. How could we? We just got here."

The room went silent. Fergus folded his arms across his chest and leaned back in his chair, tipping it against the wall. His eyes narrowed. He looked directly at us. Then he said, "Kill the woman."

Chapter 6

Charlie

Until then, my thoughts had been wavering between anger, self-pity, and disbelief. Then Mitch screamed, "NO," and lunged for the man holding Aisley.

Fergus had expected us to blurt out the location of Pendragon, so he, and everyone else in the room, was taken by surprise. But the advantage of surprise wasn't going to last long, and I could see Mitch wasn't going to get there in time, so I leapt towards the startled Fergus, grabbed one of our swords and flung it, still in its scabbard, towards the man holding the knife. It spun through the air, missing Mitch by inches and, as the man swung his knife towards Aisley, hit him in the side of the head, knocking him to the ground.

Mitch was no match for the other man, who was bigger and brawnier and wearing chain mail, and who had let go of Aisley so he could meet Mitch head on. Mitch was about to get crushed, just as soon as he came within reach of the brawny knight. Luckily, when I threw the sword at the knight with the knife, Mitch's knight became distracted. As his partner fell to the floor, he turned his head to see, putting himself off-balance. At the same moment, Mitch slammed into him, driving his shoulder into the knight's chest. The two of them tumbled backward, hitting the wall with a crack and a clatter. Mitch jumped back, ready to dodge the knight when he made a grab for him, but the man merely slid to the floor, leaving behind a head-shaped dent in the hardened mud covering the stone wall.

It was over in less than a second, but it gave me time to grab the second sword by the hilt and spin around, sending the scabbard flying towards the men who were already coming at me. Turning back to Fergus, who was still leaning back in his chair, I swung the naked blade up, leaned across the table and pointed it at his throat.

From the side of the room, I heard Mitch shout. "Back off."

I glanced his way. He had the fallen man's sword in his hands and was holding it against his chest. Aisley had taken the other man's knife and was kneeling over him, with the blade to the base of his jaw.

The room went silent. Fergus's eyes blazed and I watched as his expression went from one of shock, to fear, to anger, and then to something more familiar: cunning. He may have grown older, but he was still a coward and a bully, and a man who needed to come out on top. I could practically hear his brain spinning ideas, looking for a way to pretend he had the situation under control. I knew letting him do that was the only way we were going to get out of this alive, so I didn't resist when he raised his hand and took the tip of my sword between his thumb and index finger.

"As impetuous as ever," he said, pushing the point aside. "Now put away your weapons."

I pulled the sword back but continued to hold it ready. Fergus ignored me and stood to address his men. "Stand down. There is no need for fighting."

He looked at me and gave a sly smile, but I could see remnants of panic in his eyes. He was still searching for a way out, and eyeing my sword, which was closer to him than his men were to me. Then his smile broadened. "You are either very foolish or telling the truth. While the former is certainly true, I remain unconvinced of the latter, but you must know that your very presence renders that question moot."

We all—including his men—looked at him, wondering what he was getting at.

I took a quick glance to my right. The man lying on the floor was slowly coming around. Mitch gave him his sword back and picked up his own. Aisley released her prisoner too, but kept his knife. The fact that no one was trying to kill anyone lent a strange sort of peacefulness to the room.

"The whereabouts of your friend Pendragon is no longer of concern," Fergus continued. "I grieve that he will miss his opportunity to take part in this momentous event, but the two of you …" He hesitated. "Yes, that's it. You. You and your cloak, make his participation unnecessary."

His voice became slightly strained, as if he didn't know what he was going to say until the words came out of his mouth, and they seemed to surprise him as much as everyone else. "It is you who will fulfil the prophecy," he said, gaining confidence, "and who will, therefore, accompany me as honoured guests."

"You mean prisoners," Mitch said.

"Do I allow prisoners to carry weapons," Fergus said, giving Mitch an irritated look. "King Mordred will be pleased to welcome you."

"King," I said. "Is Arthur dead?"

A murmur began behind me and ended abruptly as Fergus looked up. "No, but he has been away these many years. An absent king is no king at all. Mordred is now king, and it is he who possesses the Talisman."

I lowered my sword. Mordred was king? Unless he had changed greatly from the lying, conniving young man he had been when we first encountered him, then the country was in trouble. And, apparently, he again had the Talisman. The thought made me cold. I looked towards Mitch, who was now coming to join me, his sword in one hand, the scabbard in the other. Aisley was by his side, still holding the knife.

Fergus looked slowly around the room, taking it all in. "This is proof that God is on our side," he said, as if trying to convince himself. "You boys will help Mordred fulfil his destiny. Pendragon, I fear, has forfeited his place in history." He looked at Aisley when he said this, then abruptly lost interest in her.

"We start back immediately," he said, then looked at us and scowled. "But you cannot travel in those costumes." He faced his men, confidently in control again. "Sir Edmund, gather the others and release the townspeople. Sir Wendell, find suitable clothing for these young men."

The remaining men began preparing for travel. Relieved by the activity, the tension drained from the room.

"Sheath your swords," Fergus said. "You will carry them." Then he picked up the cloak and smiled. "And I will carry this."

Chapter 7

Mitch

We had to take our clothes off and dress in the outfits the knights brought for us. After having pounced on us, they now treated us with respect, so the clothing they stole wasn't peasant dress, but from the town's wealthier residents. This made me feel a little better because I thought rich people could afford having their clothes stolen.

We dressed in fine shirts and sturdy jackets, comfortable pants, and crafted leather boots. We even had leather belts to hang our swords from, although they were so long and heavy, they bounced against the ground when we walked.

"I will keep your possessions safe," Aisley said, glaring at the knights as she pulled my tee-shirt and a pair of Wal-Mart underwear from one of them. When she had gathered all our clothes, she laid them on the table and stood with her back to it, daring a roomful of armed men to try to take them from her. When they backed away, she came to us, hugging Charlie, and then me. "We shall meet again," she said. "And I know you will need them."

I couldn't imagine that happening, but I admired her optimism, gave her a hug back, telling her to be well. The knights, impatient to leave, urged us out the door.

By then, more than a dozen knights were in the yard, all of them on horses, with two to spare; one for each of us. We mounted and rode out of the farmyard, with Fergus, wearing our cloak, in the lead.

We left the way we had come in, riding single file along the path bordering the river, and then up the muddy track to the edge of town. In the courtyard of The Green Dragon, we met up with the others, and I was surprised to see that, counting knights, squires and pages, there were nearly forty in all.

"This is a large company to simply capture one man," I said quietly to Charlie.

Charlie nodded. "It must be really important."

Ahead of us, Fergus turned to one of his knights. "Take two men and stay behind," he told him. "Keep watch on the woman."

"Really, really important," Charlie whispered.

We rode out of Horsham, taking the Roman road to where it intersected with the larger road leading to London. We took that road south, following it until dusk began to settle, then we camped at the edge of a dense wood. In the morning, we left the road, travelling cross-country over open plains, skirting around forests, trotting single file along pathways, and occasionally making decent time on paved roads.

It seemed a slower way to travel, but Charlie and I figured it was safer in the open because they could see if anyone was sneaking up on them. It also made it harder for us to slip away, as there was no place to hide. Even in a forest, however, we wouldn't have tried to escape, and we were certain Fergus knew it, and the reason why: he had our cloak.

The travel was easy, but there was an urgency to it. We covered more than twenty miles every day, rising at dawn and not stopping until the light grew dim. Charlie and I decided it was late summer, for the days were long and the leaves on the trees were the tired green colour they display before turning in the fall. Also, the grass we travelled through was brown and, from a distance, the gentle hills looked like rolling fields of autumn wheat.

We were treated well, and the pretence that we were honoured guests was kept up, despite it being obvious that we were prisoners. We slept in our own tent, with guards standing outside. Two men also guarded Fergus's tent, and others stood guard around the fire. They were taking no chances with us, and we assumed if we had tried to sneak out of the back of the tent, we would find guards stationed there, as well.

There was nothing to do, therefore, except go along with it. We were used to travelling by horse, but we hadn't done it since we had visited in 1588, which was three years ago, so we were a little out of practice and we had saddle sores for the first few days. Every day, all day, we urged the horses onward, stopping at intervals for food and rest, and in the evenings, the horses were bedded down, cared for, fed, and guarded.

We ate well, and were invited to dine with the leaders in Fergus's tent, but we preferred to take our meals by the fire with the rest of the company. This wasn't just so we could avoid Fergus, it was warmer by the fire, and during the meals, the men talked.

Surprisingly, they talked about us, and seemed awed that we were in their company. We were, it seemed, legends, and like most legends, the stories grew with the telling, and the versions they told had us braver, more resourceful, more cunning, and bigger, and our adventures sounded more exciting than what had really happened. The men told the tales enthusiastically, and looked to us for authentication, which we willingly supplied.

The stories included the Talisman, and how we were its Guardians, and had slain the dragon, and saved the Talisman for King Arthur. Somehow—though our exploits in those stories were brave indeed—they left out the part where we won the Talisman, and our cloak, back from Mordred in a jousting match, not to mention omitting the fact that Fergus had taken us prisoner. But they also talked about other events, telling of their own exploits and, most importantly, what it was they were doing.

That final part came late, after they had drunk a little wine, and they always spoke in quiet voices. Sometimes, we pretended to be groggy ourselves, to encourage them to speak more freely. In this way, we discovered that their search for Pendragon was a matter of some urgency. They had raced to Horsham to find him, and now were racing back with us. A great victory, Fergus called it, but not all his men agreed.

"There'll be trouble," a brawny knight said to his companion late one evening. We had been travelling several days by then, and with each passing night, the men grew bolder in their opinions and looser with their talk.

The other man raised his wine goblet in a toast. "To the Guardians, and the Cloak," he said. "King Mordred will be more than pleased."

The brawny knight shook his head and stared into the fire. "No, Mordred wanted Pendragon for a reason. It will not go well for Lord Fergus when he returns without him."

"Why so morose? The Guardians will fulfil Mordred's destiny. They have the cloak, that will give them—"

"You forget," the brawny knight continued, looking around to see if anyone was lurking nearby, "King Mordred's position is tenuous. That is why he wanted Pendragon. Having the Guardians may not displease him, but not having Pendragon will, I fear, displease him greatly."

His companion, refusing to be drawn into his friend's sombre mood, slapped him on the back and laughed. "Just so long as he isn't displeased with us."

Another night, as we camped within sight of the circle of stones they call Stonehenge, we listened to a different group whose whispers, thanks to many flagons of beer, sounded more like quiet shouting.

"To the coming battle, and glory," a short, portly knight proclaimed, holding his ale mug aloft. A bushy, foam-covered moustache beneath his bulbous nose seemed to flap as he spoke, and I realized, with some dread, that he was the knight Charlie had thrown his sword at, the one he had stopped from killing Aisley.

His companions were less enthusiastic. "If a battle is to come," said one, "I will fight, but I will find no glory in killing our brother knights." He took a swig of ale and ran the back of his hand across his mouth.

"Rest your minds," a third knight said. He was tall and barrel-chested, with curly, black hair and a short beard, and I recognized him as the knight I had slammed into the wall. I wondered how friendly they would be towards us if they found us alone, like we were now. I nudged Charlie and pointed, and he nodded, letting me know he recognized them too. Then we pretended to sleep again, as the knight continued, "there will be no battle."

The other knight shook his head and stared into the fire. "But our quest was a failure, we were to—"

"Mind your words, Sir Barlow," the tall knight said. "To speak of failure besmirches Lord Fergus, and many would find offense in such talk."

"Not the least Lord Fergus," the portly one said.

The men snickered.

"All I say is," continued Barlow, "if we return without Pendragon, King Mordred's plan for a peaceful outcome will be compromised."

I heard a sword sliding from its scabbard and saw a blade, held aloft, by the portly knight, glinting in the firelight. "If there is to be a battle, I say let it come. Let the bravest take the day, and if death comes for us, it will be a death with honour."

Then Sir Barlow stepped forward and looked down at the shorter knight's face. "Will your widow be comforted by those words, Sir Alwyn? Will my widow, or will Sir Leland's widow, find comfort in our bravery while we all lay, unmoving, on the field?"

"You speak treason—"

"I speak truth.

They faced each other, one holding a leather cup

and the other a sword. The tall knight, Sir Leland, stepped between them. "Put away your sword, Sir Alwyn, and save your bravado for battle." Then he turned to the other. "And curb your tongue, Sir Barlow, such talk spreads disquiet among the men."

"The men are already disquieted," Barlow said. "They know as well as I do that if Mordred and Arthur clash, it will be slaughter."

"Then we must hope King Mordred can broker peace."

Alwyn sheathed his sword. "Knights do not wish for peace," he muttered. "They seek glory, and the field of Camlann is where I hope to find it."

More arguing followed. We kept listening, pretending to be asleep until we really were. Sometime later, I was awakened by a foot nudging my side. A pair of leather boots stood in front of me. Beyond was the fire, now reduced to embers. "What?" I asked the boots.

"Bed for the pair of you," a voice said. I looked up, beyond the boots into the bearded face of Sir Leland. "Tomorrow will come early, and end late."

Next to me, Sir Alwyn nudged Charlie awake, though it seemed more like he kicked him.

"Hey!" Charlie said.

Alwyn laughed. "Up, you whelp."

I rose to my feet, the sleep slowly clearing from my head. Aching and shivering from the cold, we stumbled to our tent and wrapped ourselves in our blankets.

I started to drift off as soon as I settled on the cushions, but Charlie remained awake.

"Did you hear what Alwyn said?"

I groaned and tried to ignore him.

"He said he wanted to fight on the field of Camlann."

"What of it," I mumbled.

Charlie sighed. "A year or so ago, I read a book about King Arthur. Camlann is his final battle. It's the place where he dies."

Chapter 8

Charlie

We were awakened before sunrise by the clanking of armour and weapons and peered out of the tent expecting to see a battle. Instead, we saw a group of pages, sitting in the murky dawn, polishing breastplates, gauntlets, and swords around the rekindled fire. The three knights—Sir Alwyn, Sir Leland, and Sir Barlow—were with them, sitting cross-legged on the ground, and eating from wooden bowls.

When they saw us, they made us join them, then they made us take off our clothes so the pages could clean and press them. They gave us robes to wear, but they were drafty and thin as hospital gowns, so we had to huddle by the fire to keep warm because more pages were already taking our tent down.

"Before the sun sets this day," Sir Leland said, noting our discomfort, "you will be safe and warm within the camp of King Mordred."

"And near to our enemy," Sir Alwyn said, "Arthur and his band of traitors."

Leland turned to Alwyn. "Arthur is not our enemy, nor are his men traitors. They are brother knights, with whom we seek peace."

Alwyn glared at him, but said nothing.

The silence grew heavy, so I concentrated on my breakfast: a concoction of mushy oatmeal with some leftover meat mixed into it. It looked like someone already ate it, but it was hot and filling and surprisingly tasty. For the next hour, until the sky lightened, we ate, drank small beer—which is beer without much alcohol in it—and watched the pages help the knights on with their armour. When they finally returned our clothes, they were in much the same condition as when we had handed them over, but at least they didn't smell as bad.

When full light came, the squires helped the knights mount their horses. We mounted ours and the little group, numbering eight in all, trotted out of the camp, with Fergus in the lead, leaving the others behind to clean up the camp and follow later. It seemed an odd thing to do, but Mitch thought that maybe Fergus wanted it to look like he had completed his mission with only a few men, rather than a small army.

Fergus, we noted, was no longer wearing our cloak. It was, instead, carefully packed into a leather bag, carried by Sir Leland, who rode just behind Fergus. Next to Leland was Sir Barlow, carrying Fergus's battle standard. We rode behind them, with a page on either side of us and Sir Alwyn bringing up the rear. Fergus was taking no chances on us making a break for it.

We rode down tracks and lanes, and over low hills covered with knee-high grass, always expecting to find whatever it was we were heading for just beyond the next rise, but noon came, and we were still riding, and riding fast. We covered nearly twenty miles in the first half of the day, stopping only occasionally to rest the horses and take food and drink. During the afternoon, the clouds that had hidden the sky drifted away, and we rode into the uncomfortable glare of the setting sun. We stopped one last time, as the sun neared the horizon, so the pages could brush up Fergus's armour. Then we moved on. A short time later, from the summit of a broad hill, we finally saw Mordred's camp.

I say camp, but what we had left that morning was a camp, what we were heading towards was an army. It spread across the grassy plain, forming a huge stain on the pristine landscape, a writhing mass of men and horses, dotted with tents and flags and battle standards, all covered in a haze of smoke from hundreds of fires.

But that wasn't all we could see. Some distance away, separated by a wide sweep of open ground and a narrow river, was another army. They might have been two halves of a single army, but the line of men at the edge of each camp, keeping watch across the river towards the other army, hinted that these were adversaries rather than allies.

From this distance, Arthur's army didn't look as large as Mordred's, but it was large enough to keep Mordred from wanting to attack. I recalled the conversations we had overheard, and now knew why some of the knights wanted to avoid battle: the carnage that would result if these two armies clashed would be unimaginable. Unmatched even by the horrific scenes we had witnessed at the battle of Stamford Bridge.

Both Mordred and Arthur must have known this,

or an attack would have happened by now. The armies must have marched to meet and then settled in, either waiting for an advantage or trying to negotiate peace. I wondered if our being taken prisoner, and the search for Pendragon, was Mordred's way of trying to break the stalemate.

As we approached, men on the outskirts stopped what they were doing and began to cheer. Soon the sound spread through the camp, deafening us. We walked the horses carefully through the throng that had gathered around us. Fergus waved and greeted them like a conquering hero, as the rest of us struggled to keep up.

Inside the camp, the grass had been trampled flat, and the ground felt rock-hard beneath our horse's hooves. We passed by tents, sagging under the weight of time, and pits filled with the ashes of many fires. Here and there, clusters of pages sat cross-legged on the ground, polishing bits of already gleaming armour, while the knights, wearing simple shirts and loose pants, walked among them, inspecting their work, and cuffing those whose efforts did not measure up. And everywhere, the air was thick with the smell of cooked meat and unwashed bodies.

We worked our way through the crowd, into the centre of the camp, where a large tent stood on its own. Two knights, dressed in battle armour and holding lances, stood guard outside. Above the tent, a flag bearing the image of a black dragon hung limply from a tall pole.

When we entered the clearing in front of the tent, the guards went into a battle stance and held their lances pointed at us. We came to a halt, and Fergus raised his hand in greeting. "Hail Mordred, King of the Britons, It is I, Sir Fergus, returning in victory having done his Highness's bidding."

The guards returned to their original positions. "Pass, Sir Fergus."

"Nothing like a little pomp and circumstance," Mitch whispered as we dismounted.

Sir Alwyn and the pages took our horses. The guards pulled the tent flaps aside so Fergus could enter. They followed him in, leaving the four of us outside. Sir Leland tucked the leather bag containing our cloak under one arm and stood at attention near the entrance of the tent. Barlow encouraged us to move up, so we stood either side of him, at attention, waiting to be admitted.

Then a voice came from within the tent. "Sir Fergus, returned from your quest?"

There came the sound of metal clanking as Fergus knelt. "Yes, your highness."

"Victorious, I trust?"

"Doubly so." More clanking as he rose to his feet.

"Then why is Pendragon not before me? Bring him at once."

There was a brief silence which, even through the tent, we could feel was uncomfortable.

"I have returned with prizes equal to, nay, superior to the importance of Pendragon."

Another silence, even more uncomfortable than the first. When Mordred finally spoke, it was in a low rumble moving towards a major eruption.

"You dare instruct me on the importance of

Pendragon?"

"No, your highness—"

"You believe you have special knowledge about what Pendragon can do for me?"

"No, your highness. I simply thought—"

"You do not think. I think, and you follow orders. I sent you to capture Pendragon, and you return without him, then you seek to deceive me by saying your mission was a success when, in fact, you failed." Mordred's voice rose with each syllable, until he was shouting loud enough for everyone around the tent to hear the word "failed" clearly.

Fergus cleared his throat. "I was able—"

"I wanted Pendragon. I shall have Pendragon. Did you not capture the woman? Could you not torture the information out of her? Or did she defeat you as well?"

"No," Fergus said, "I mean, yes, we found the woman, and then—"

"And then you failed to make her talk. How many failures can you achieve in a single mission?"

"Your Highness, there is—"

"There is nothing! I have searched this kingdom, I have searched other lands, my spies have searched the enemy camp, and they found nothing. So, he must be in the only place I have not searched, at his home, hiding behind his mother's skirt. I sent you to bring him to me, but you return with nothing. I want Pendragon, and you have brought me nothing."

By now Mordred was screeching. I imagined him red-faced and beating his fists in the air like a two-year-old who'd been denied an ice cream cone.

44

"I have a gift for you," Fergus blurted when Mordred drew a breath.

Leland took this to be his cue. Clutching the bag, he lurched forward and disappeared into the tent.

"What is the meaning of this," Mordred screeched. "Who is this man? I gave no permission—"

"Your gift—"

"You think to excuse your failure with trinkets? I am a king, not a broken-hearted harlot. This insult will—"

During the tirade, me and Mitch slowly backed away from the tent. Behind us, Barlow was practically at the edge of the clearing. Then there was sudden silence and we stopped moving backward and moved forward again, listening.

For nearly a minute, no one said anything, then Mordred spoke, his voice soft and edged with awe. "Is this …"

"Yes, m'lord," Fergus said, his voice cautious but gaining confidence.

"Arthur's cloak. How did you … did you kill him?" The final words were uttered in a tone of hopeful glee.

"It is not Arthur's," Fergus said. Then hastily added, "It is the other."

No one said anything for a few moments, then Mordred spoke. "The youths? The conniving, traitorous youths?"

"The Guardians," Fergus said. "They are waiting outside."

"This is their cloak?"

"It is. And with them and their cloak, Pendragon's assistance is no longer necessary."

"You school me again on what is necessary?" Mordred said, his voice regaining its former menace. "You believe you know better than your King?"

"No, most certainly not, my Lord."

"Then why do you pretend to think? Why do you dare to tell me Pendragon is not important? Why would you countermand my wishes?"

"I would not, I did not. I have not given up the search for Pendragon—"

"But you are here, and Pendragon is not."

"I left spies. The woman will betray him when she feels it is safe—"

"The woman?" Mordred said, his voice rising again. "What use can she ..." Then his voice trailed off. "The cloak. Give it to me."

Rustling and clanking as Fergus helped Mordred put on our cloak.

"Returned to you at long last," Fergus said. "Your destiny is assured."

"Don't tell me what I already know," Mordred snapped. "Stay silent, all of you, I must think."

The sounds of the camp were now all I could hear. Inside the tent, all was silent. I looked at Mitch. He glanced over his shoulder at Barlow, then back at me, and shrugged. I shook my head and we both returned to staring at the tent flaps, waiting to be called.

My feet ached, and dusk was approaching, by the time Mordred spoke again.

"You did well, Sir Fergus. You and your brave

knights. This cloak does give me an advantage. With it, the Talisman, and the Guardians, I have all required to fulfil the prophecy. There is no need for battle. No need to kill ten thousand knights to acquire that which I already possess."

Fergus cleared his throat.

"That is welcome news, indeed, your highness."

"Except," Mordred continued, "for one thing. I could ride to the Isle of Avalon now and be done with all by morning, were it not for the treachery of my father. He left me in charge. He made me King. I have every right to the Talisman, and the prophecy."

"But you remain king," Fergus said. "Arthur's words mean nothing."

"Not his words," Mordred said, "his presence. You may call me King, the people may call me King, but with Arthur returned, and claiming he never left his throne, the only words that matter are his. Until Arthur himself proclaims me King, I can do nothing. And that is why I need Pendragon."

"Your Highness, you have—"

"I have nothing," Mordred said, already in full-rage mode. "You cannot see. Only I can see. Pendragon is the key to getting what I need. These trappings, they are dust and ash unless I can extract the words, 'You are King' from Arthur's lips. And Pendragon is the key that will unlock those words."

"Your Highness, I … I …"

"You, you what?" Mordred screamed. Then he drew a breath and turned the volume down. "You left spies, did you say?"

"Yes, your Highness."

"Then Pendragon may already be in your possession."

"It is possible."

"And if he is not, the woman herself might do. She and anyone else dear to Pendragon. Would your spies have followed her if she went to visit a wife or child of Pendragon?"

"They would follow her every move."

"Excellent. Then return straightaway. Bring the woman, and anyone she may have revealed, to me at all speed."

"Yes, your highness. I will leave at first light."

"You will leave now. You will take five men. You will ride fast and hard, gather your prisoners and return with great haste."

"Certainly, your highness," Fergus said. "I shall—"

"Why are you not on your horse yet?" Mordred shouted. "Leave me, both of you. And send in the Guardians."

Chapter 9

Mitch

Fergus burst from the tent, followed by Leland, their faces white, and Fergus's eyes wide with panic. He brushed past us without a word. Leland paused only long enough to say, "The King requests your presence," before stumbling after Fergus.

Charlie looked at me. "Should we just go in?"

I took a step closer. "Maybe we ought to knock first."

"What should we do when we see him?"

"I don't know, but try not getting him angry?"

Charlie huffed. "Why not?"

I didn't get to answer. The tent flaps parted, held aside by two knights. One of them said, "You may enter." So, we stepped through the doorway.

The light was getting dim outside, but inside the tent was bright. The two knights flanked us, and we moved forward, heading towards the back of the tent. It was large, supported by wooden beams thick as telephone poles, many with flaming torches attached. Cushioned seats and oak tables—some covered with papers, others with bowls of food—were scattered amid the columns. A big chair sat at the far end, nearly concealed by smoke from the torches. Sitting on the chair was Mordred.

"It this how you greet your King? Kneel."

I didn't see who shouted the command, but there was no arguing with it. We both touched a knee to the ground and bowed our heads for a few seconds. When we thought we'd been submissive enough, we stood.

"Come closer," Mordred said.

The chair he sat on was made of dark wood with fancy carvings and spires jutting from the back. The cushions on the seat, back, and arms were of a dark blue fabric, the same colour as our cloak, which Mordred had wrapped around him. The cloak's collar was clasped at his throat by the Talisman.

Mordred leaned forward. His thin, white face, flanked by black hair and topped with a small gold crown, seemed to float in the smoky light. We were barely ten feet away when our guards brought us to a halt. Other guards stood on either side of Mordred's chair, and more were scattered about the room.

Mordred peered at us. "It is you," he said, leaning back onto the cushions. "The Travellers, the Guardians, returned to restore the cloak to its rightful owner. I should thank you for that, you have saved me much bother."

"It's not your cloak," Charlie said. I felt myself go cold, but I didn't dare try to punch him in the arm to make him shut up. The guards might think I was attempting an attack.

But Mordred didn't explode, he merely looked at us with a puzzled expression. "You are mistaken. Recall that I won this cloak from you in fair combat."

"What I recall," Charlie continued, "is that we beat you, and won our cloak back, as well as the Talisman."

This time Mordred did explode. "False tales," he shouted, leaping to his feet, "false, scurrilous tales. If such slander offends my ear again, those who said it will have their tongues ripped from their mouths." I noticed that, as he said this, he was looking around the room at his knights, not at us.

To my relief, Charlie clamped his mouth shut and didn't respond. Mordred glared at us, then sat, and drummed his fingers on the arm of his chair. Gradually, his scowl softened. His lips twitched into a smile. He stopped drumming his fingers. "You picked an auspicious time to return," he said. "Many years I searched for you. With your strange manners and dress, you should have been easy to find, but you disappeared into the air. And now, just when I need your services, you return, bringing my cloak with you. This is surely proof that God is, indeed, with me."

He stood, looking beyond us to address the room. "Do you not see this as Divine blessing, a confirmation that we will prevail?"

"Our cause is just," the knights responded, nearly in unison.

Mordred waved his hand in a dismissive gesture and looked around the room. "You may depart. I and our new comrades have much to discuss."

One of the knights standing by Mordred's chair hesitated. "Your Highness, would you have us disarm them before we depart?"

"They are friends," Mordred said. "We have nothing to fear from them." He looked at us, and our swords. "They will be hungry," he said to no one in particular. "Bring them table. I shall watch them dine."

Knights gathered food and plates and arranged them on one of the tables. Then they carried it to the middle of the tent.

"Sit," Mordred said, rising. His guards encouraged us towards the table while two knights carried Mordred's chair, following him as he came to the table and sat at one end. Smaller, lower chairs were set out for us at the opposite end. We tried to sit but the swords made it awkward.

One of Mordred's guards stood behind us. "You may wish to remove your swords," he said, then leaned forward, lowering his voice. "Dining with weapons is not only uncomfortable, it is impolite. You would not wish to offend your king."

We took off our swords and laid them on a table near the side of the tent. There was no point in protesting. In truth, I was glad to be free of it; it was heavy and awkward, and I hadn't planned on stabbing him anyway, so there was no reason to keep it. Once we were disarmed and reseated, the guards left with the rest of the knights, leaving us alone with Mordred.

"Eat," Mordred said.

We looked at the table. We had fine plates and goblets. What we didn't have was any silverware. Not a fork, knife or even a teaspoon was to be seen. Bowls of meat, bread, and cheese were nearby, all of them cut into small pieces we could pick up and eat.

"Are you not hungry?" Mordred asked.

"We're, um, waiting for you," Charlie said. "It's

rude to start eating before the host."

Mordred gave a quick laugh. "Please," he said, "eat." He waved a hand towards us as encouragement. I picked up a piece of bread and put some meat on it to make a tiny sandwich. "One should only eat with one's equals. Since I have no equals, I dine alone."

Charlie took some cheese and meat, and stole a quick look at our swords lying, not far away, but too far to think about making a grab for them. Mordred saw his look. He said nothing, but moments later he leaned back in his chair and idly reached under the cloak to pull out a thin dagger. He made a pretence of cleaning his fingernails with the point and when he saw us looking, he smiled sheepishly.

"A vanity," he said, admiring his nails. Then he held the dagger up, turning it so the blade flashed in the torchlight. "I shouldn't use this for grooming. It's so sharp, I might accidentally draw blood."

We both kept our eyes on the food and off our swords.

"And so, my friends," Mordred said as we continued eating, "what is it that drew you here? The truth, please." He touched the tip of the dagger to his chin, and then rested it on his lap, his hand still clutching the handle.

I looked at Charlie, who shrugged and said, "Good question."

"I will not ask again," Mordred said, his voice harder now. "Why did you return?"

Charlie ate another piece of meat. "Good question," he muttered. I looked at Mordred, who either hadn't heard or chose to ignore him.

"Answer," Mordred said, rising to his feet. "I am your king and I command you to answer the question. Why are you here?"

In that moment, I saw the Mordred we used to know. The young knight, full of self-doubt, making up for his lack of authority with bluster and bullying. His bluster was rising now. He had us, and the cloak, and the Talisman, yet he was frightened. Our presence, while an advantage to him, could also mean that forces beyond his control were working against him.

This is what he wanted to know: were we here to help him, or Arthur.

I squared my shoulders and looked into his eyes. "We were called."

Mordred froze. The knuckles on his hand holding the dagger turned white. "Called?"

"Yes," I said. "A summons came to us, in our world, and we answered. That's why we are here."

"Who called you?"

I struggled to maintain my gaze. It wasn't a question I was expecting. In truth, it wasn't a question I had ever thought about. Charlie and I got the gifts, we used the cloak, and we went. We never thought about it before we went, nor did we discuss it when we returned. Our return generally involved long naps over the following days, and a few weeks of secretly discussing things that had happened, but then we usually forgot about the travels, and the cloak, and the gifts, until the next summer came around.

I guess we knew, on some level, that we were

being called, but it never occurred to either of us to wonder who was issuing the summons. It certainly wasn't Granddad. He couldn't know what it was he was doing. We always went to Pendragon's house, but that was simply because we knew where it was. Mr. Merwyn, or Mendel or whatever the old Druid was known as these days, he always seemed to expect us, but did he call us? Those were the common threads in all our adventures, along with the cloak, and the fact that we always ended up doing something with—

"Do not try my patience," Mordred said, regaining his bluster. "Who summoned you?"

The words came out of my mouth before I could think. "The Talisman," I said. Then I realized they were true. "It is the Talisman that calls us," I continued, before Mordred could bark again. "When the Land is in peril, the Talisman calls us from our world, and we answer."

As I spoke, Mordred slowly lowered himself into his seat. I realized that, for the moment, I had the advantage. I decided to push it.

"We come when there is need of us, when the Land needs the wisdom of the Talisman."

I stopped to gage Mordred's reaction. Charlie nudged me in the side with his elbow. "Give it a rest, Mitch," he whispered. "You're going to drive him crazy."

Mordred said nothing, but he stopped staring at me and, instead, looked above me, his face dreamy, and I knew he was spinning this revelation to his advantage.

"If you come for the Talisman," he said at length, "then you come to help me."

I decided not to argue. If he thought we were on his side, we'd have a better chance of getting our cloak back.

"In this struggle, we are brothers," he continued. "The Land is, indeed, in peril, and I intend to save it."

He stood and slowly raised an arm. It rose with the cloak draped over it and the dagger pointing our way. "With your help, and this cloak, and the Talisman, my Kingdom will be secured. There will be no battle, and my subjects will be blessed with an Eternal King."

Charlie cleared his throat. "Are you sure—"

"Yes," I said, nudging him again. "If there is a battle coming, we will do all we can to stop it."

Mordred lowered his arm and sheathed the dagger. "And the Talisman, the sacred stone that called you here, will guide you." He touched the golden clasp at his throat that held the Talisman. "You are the Guardians. The Talisman speaks to you, as it speaks to me. It tells me I am to be King of this land for eternity. Allow it to tell you how to help me. Come. Touch it and see."

Chapter 10

Charlie

We walked to the end of the table where Mordred sat, stroking the Talisman clasped at his throat, and I felt a sense of dread rising from my stomach. Mordred didn't mind touching the Talisman. I didn't know what it told him, but I knew it confirmed his darkest desires, because that's what it did to everyone who acquired it by theft. It would tell him what he wanted to hear, and he would believe with unshakable faith. It would seduce him, and he would be unable to resist. But the Talisman never told us anything good. We only saw the dark side, the ugly side, the side that told us the truth. And the truth was never pretty.

We stood near Mordred, on opposite sides of the table. When he saw our heads were nearly level with his, he stood, towering over us. I glanced down and saw that his throne was on a platform, so he would always be taller than anyone else. We waited, looking at the Talisman.

It was flawless, so smooth it didn't look like a stone, but more like an opening into a dark world. It was locked inside a gold band with plates on either side that were attached to the collar of our robe with long, thick pins. Mordred flicked a latch, and the top of the band swung open, releasing the Talisman. He held it in his hand, running his long fingers over the shiny surface. Then he held it out to Mitch.

Mitch took it, and held it in both hands, looking into its surface. After a few seconds, his jaw went slack and his eyes glazed over, and I knew the Talisman was speaking to him.

Moments later, he raised his head and lowered the Talisman. Mordred looked at him expectantly.

"I saw water," Mitch said. "A wide stretch of water, with a mountain rising from it."

Mordred clasped his hands, making a single clap. "Avalon," he said. "Of course. And we are there? You and I, together?"

"A boat," Mitch said. "We were on a boat."

"Yes," Mordred said, "that's right, that's absolutely right." I could tell there was more Mitch wanted to say, but Mordred didn't want to hear it. He pointed at me, "Now you."

Mitch handed me the Talisman. I held it by the edges, my stomach in knots, and looked into it. Looking into the Talisman was like looking into the future. It always showed us something, something significant, but it never explained what it was or why it was important, and I wasn't sure if I wanted to see what the future had in store for us. I felt my fingers tingle where they touched the stone. Its surface looked cold and deep, and I felt as if I was being pulled into the blackness. And I saw fire.

It raged all around me, but I still felt cold, and as I looked into the fire, I was gripped by such an overwhelming sense of loss that I was afraid I would start crying. I snapped my head up, breathing hard and shivering. But my eyes returned to the Talisman. It still burned, but the flames no longer frightened me. They soothed, they provided comfort, peace. Regretfully, I pulled my eyes away.

"Fire," I said, answering Mordred's unasked question.

Mordred took the Talisman and smoothed the front of his cloak—our cloak—with the flat of his hand. "I suppose," he said, with diminished enthusiasm, "it could be a real or metaphorical fire, for no one knows what will happen when the Talisman is seated in its place in the Temple. Fire may well play a part. But the outcome is certain." He placed the Talisman back in the ring and closed it, locking the Talisman in, then put his fists on his hips, making the cloak spread like wings. "All is as it should be. You will fulfil the prophecy as soon as the final piece is in place. Until then, you will be my guests."

He sat down and waved a hand, dismissing us, and called for the guards.

Four knights entered the tent in a rush. They stopped when it was clear that we weren't attacking Mordred. Then they stood, looking from Mordred to us and back to Mordred, wondering what to do.

"These young men are our guests," Mordred told them. "See to their comfort and safety."

"Yeah, safety," I muttered to Mitch as we were led away. "That means keeping us locked up."

"Young men," Mordred said, as we were halfway to the door. "Retrieve your swords."

With the knights standing close by, we got our swords and strapped them around our waists. All the while, Mordred kept his eye on us.

"Young men," he said again, when we were ready to leave a second time, "I cannot continue to refer to you as Young Men. Remind us of your names."

Mitch faced him and stood straight, as if at attention. "My name is Mitch."

I stood next to him. "And I am Charlie."

To our surprise, Mordred rose and came towards us, the dagger back in his hand.

"Well then, Mitch and Charlie, you are about to perform a most sacred task, and I cannot have you doing that with such names." He stood before us, the dagger held pointing straight up. "Kneel."

I went white, certain he was going to kill us. Running was out of the question, as was attacking him. With the four guards standing so close, we'd be dead before we got our swords out. So, we knelt.

Instead of stabbing us, Mordred touched the dagger to Mitch's shoulder, and then to mine. Then he stepped back and said, "Rise, Sir Mitch, rise, Sir Charlie."

We stood. The dagger disappeared beneath our cloak, and Mordred returned to his throne and sat, a satisfied smile on his face. "All is as it should be now. You may go."

We knew the drill, so without being told, or touched, we backed up a few steps, forcing the knights to jump out of our way, while Mordred nodded approvingly. Then we turned and walked away, flanked on both sides, and in front and behind, by the knights.

As we left the tent and entered the dark, cool

night, I stepped close to Mitch.

"Remember how people we met on our adventures kept calling us knights," I whispered. "Do you suppose this is why?"

Mitch shook his head. "I don't know. I don't feel like a knight. Do you?"

Chapter 11

Mitch

We were put in a tent that appeared to have been set up for us while we had been with Mordred. It was large—not as large as Mordred's, but twice the size of the ones used by the knights—and comfortable, with beds, chairs, a table, oil lamps, and a fire out front tended by two pages who, apparently, were to be our servants.

The beds were basic camp beds, just a mat on the ground, but they were topped with soft mattresses, thick blankets, and pillows filled with goose down instead of chicken feathers. Flagons of ale and wine, and fancy, metal goblets for drinking, sat on the table, along with a large wooden bowl filled with water, which we assumed was to wash in, not to drink.

The tent was also well-guarded, but we sort of expected that.

"It's not the worst prison cell we've had to endure," Charlie said as we sat down on our beds. He had to whisper, because the pages were still inside with us, filling and lighting the oil lamps.

"At least we can pretend to be free," I whispered back, "and we're close to our cloak, and the Talisman."

"Yeah, but how do we get them?"

I kept silent until the pages left, then said, "I don't know, but at least we can keep an eye on it, and watch for an opportunity."

"There won't be one. Mordred is paranoid. He's surrounded by guards. He has us surrounded by guards. We're as trapped as if we were in the Tower of London."

I laid back on my bed. It was warm and soft and suddenly I felt more like sleeping than arguing about what to do.

"Well, if all we can do is sit and wait, at least we'll be comfortable."

Charlie stood and began to pace. "I don't call this comfortable. We're in very real danger. Mordred wants us to do something, and we have to pretend, not only that we will do it, but that we know what it is. If he thinks we're of no use to him, that will be the end of us. And he's pretending that we're the answer to his problem, yet he's still desperate to find Pendragon."

I sighed. "Then we'll have to keep watch and see if we can find an advantage."

"For how long? There's a battle coming."

"Mordred is trying to avoid a battle," I said. "It may never come. We have to hope for the best."

"But history tells us it does come," Charlie said, slumping down on his bed. If it really is the Battle of Camlann, then it happens. It already did happen, hundreds of years in our past, so we can't stop it."

"Then we need to be ready. So, watch and wait and—"

"Yeah, I know, hope for the best." He pulled a

blanket over himself and finally settled down, leaving me wide awake and worrying.

◆

The next morning, when the pages saw we were awake they brought us breakfast and served it on the table. It was cold in the tent, though, so we took it outside and ate by the fire. This didn't please the pages.

"Sires," the toffee-haired one said, "you cannot eat out here like servants." He was little more than a boy, though he claimed to be eleven, almost as old as we were when we first visited. He had smooth, pale skin, a round face, and lived a cliché by having a pageboy haircut. He told us his name was Walter, and after I told him we preferred to sit by the fire he stood silent, as if uncertain of what to do. Then he looked at Mordred's tent, about a hundred yards away, and back at us, and back at Mordred's tent.

"Mordred has ordered you to keep us inside," I said, "and you're afraid he'll think you've disobeyed. Is that it?"

"You are not prisoners," he said, a little too quickly, "but there are protocols." He pronounced the word protocol as if he had just learned it that morning.

"Does the protocol ever allow us to go outside?" Charlie asked, through a mouthful of food.

"Certainly," Walter said. "But for knights to sit by the fire, eating like peasants, it's …"

I could have told him I had seen plenty of knights

doing it, but instead I said, "Mordred won't like it, will he? And that will make things go badly for you. Is that right?"

With that, the other page, the one with the black hair and dark eyes and brooding nature, who had been resolutely tending the fire, stood up and faced us. "Mordred is a great king. He wants only the best for you, for his people, for us. He is wise and merciful." He talked like an infomercial and flexed his hands as he spoke. "You should not speak ill of him, especially as he is showing you such kindness."

"By holding us prisoner?" Charlie asked. "That's a strange way of showing kindness."

Both the pages turned red, Walter with embarrassment, the other with rage. I stood and grabbed Charlie by an arm. "If it pleases you then, we'll eat inside."

"Hey!" Charlie said, shaking me off.

"I think it's for the best," I said. "It would be rude not to accept our host's hospitality."

I went into the tent, hoping Charlie would follow. Seconds later he did. He thumped his bowl down on the table and slumped into a chair.

"What was that all about?"

"We have to pick our battles."

"But this battle picked us."

"Yes, but we don't have to fight it. If those pages are to be our guards, I'd rather have them on our side. I don't want to make enemies of them."

"Why not?" Charlie asked, taking another mouthful of porridge.

"For one thing, they make our meals. If we get them angry, they might piss in our food."

Charlie spit porridge back into the bowl. "Ewww."

"They won't have done it yet," I said, "but you'd better check your lunch carefully."

Charlie pushed his bowl away. "I don't feel hungry anymore. I don't think I'm going to eat again, ever."

I finished my breakfast, while Charlie glared at me, then pushed my bowl away. "Let's see if we're allowed to go out now," I said.

Charlie frowned. "I thought you didn't want to antagonize them."

"I don't. But they're claiming we're not prisoners, so they'll have some explaining to do if they try to prevent us from taking a look around."

We left the tent and found Walter tending the fire. The other page was nowhere to be seen.

"We're going for a walk," I said.

Walter looked uncertain. He glanced at Mordred's tent and then scanned around the camp.

"Are we allowed?" Charlie asked.

"Yes, certainly," Walter said, "but it's a big camp. You might get lost. You really should have a guide with you."

"Will you guide us, then?" I asked him.

"I ..." he glanced around again, "I have duties."

"Then we'll leave you to them," Charlie said.

"Don't worry," I told him. "We won't go far."

As we walked away, Walter looked so wretched I almost felt sorry for him.

"Where are we going?" Charlie asked.

"Just anywhere," I said, "but keep your eyes open."

"For what?"

"For Malcolm, or Mr. Merwyn, or whatever the Druid is calling himself now. He seems to pop up when we're in trouble, and if we ever needed help, it's now."

We walked further from our tent, looking at groups of men sitting by fires, but none of them had long, grey beards or a scar around their right eye.

The sky remained overcast and the air still, which kept the smoke from the many fires low, shrouding the camp in a fog that nearly choked us. We hadn't gone far before we decided to turn back. Then we heard someone calling us. I turned, expecting to see a familiar figure dressed in a white robe, but instead saw Sir Leland and the dark-haired page sprinting towards us.

"Sir Mitch, Sir Charlie," he called. We stopped and, once the page saw us, he let Leland go ahead while he returned to our tent. "I must apologize," he said when he caught up with us, "I am to be your guide. If you wish to see the camp, I can show it to you."

Charlie leaned close. "So much for not being prisoners.

Chapter 12

Charlie

Even though Leland was there to guard us, he turned out to be a pretty good guide. He led us from campfire to campfire, where we met more of the knights. They knew we were the Guardians and they treated us like celebrities, and called us Sir Charlie and Sir Mitch, which made my skin crawl.

They were all nice enough but, like Leland, they spoke carefully, almost condescendingly, like we were New York Ranger fans at a Pittsburgh Penguin game, and they didn't want to offend us and start a riot.

The camp was such a confusion of tents, fire pits, bored men, piles of weapons, and intertwining tracks that, within an hour, I realized Walter was right: we would never have found our way back. It made me glad that Leland had been sent to mind us, but I still wasn't happy with the idea.

After a while, I tuned Leland out as he continued to give us a running commentary on our tour, and instead followed Mitch's lead and began looking around for the old Druid. I was surprised that he hadn't turned up along with our pages. He seemed to be good at impersonating a cook. But there was no one around that even looked like him. Everywhere we went there were men, men, and more men, and all of them had broad shoulders, thick necks and brawny arms. They were peaceful, relaxed, and occasionally jolly, but there was an undercurrent of tension.

Near noon, Leland brought us back to our tent, where Walter and his buddy had prepared a lunch of cooked meat and hunks of bread. It wasn't something they could have easily pissed in, but I gave it a good sniff, nonetheless.

After lunch, Leland returned with horses and we rode out to the front lines, where we saw the source of the unease. Here, at the edge of the dormant conflict, the threat, and consequences, of war became evident.

Scattered along the line facing the river and Arthur's camp, were heavily armed men, most with swords or large spears. Spread among them were huge battle machines—catapults and something they called a war machine.

The catapults were built on wheeled platforms that had been staked to the ground. They were huge and heavy, with ropes and winches and a big arm topped with a pocket for the payload. I assumed they would be loaded with rocks, as there were piles of cannonball-sized boulders next to each one, along with about eight men who I presumed would be needed to load, prepare, and fire it.

But much bigger than the catapults were the war machines, strange devices with long arms on a pivot. The wheeled platforms holding these devices were three times the size of the ones for the catapults. Huge triangles made of logs rose from the sides of the platforms, held stable by iron bars attached to their tips. Massive rods of wood—thick at one end and thin at the other—pointed into the air, pierced by the iron bars about a third of the way up from the heavy end, which caused the rods to stand straight, their slender lengths pointing into the sky like skinny flagpoles. Each rod had a rope and leather sling dangling from it. Stacked nearby were crude hay-bales that someone had, apparently, painted black.

"Look to the fore."

The shout came from one of the lookouts closest to the river, and it sent men scattering in all directions. Some squeezed under the platforms of the machines they were manning, others hid behind them, and the rest just ran as fast as they could.

"This way," Leland said, tugging his reins.

We followed his lead, galloping away from the river. Behind us, I heard a thud, then Leland raised his hand and we stopped. As we returned to the front, it became clear what had happened.

One of the catapults had been hit with something. Two dazed men sat on the ground next to it and, scattered over the catapult, and the men, and the ground, was a mass of blackened straw. It started just in front of the catapult and fanned out in a "V", covering the catapult and the men who had sheltered next to it.

"Anyone hurt?" Leland asked as we drew near.

The men shook their heads, climbed to their feet, and tried to brush the straw away. I saw then that it wasn't paint, but tar. They brushed off what they could and checked the catapult while other men began gathering up the scattered straw.

"This requires an answer," Leland said, gazing

upward. He wasn't looking towards the river, but off to the side, and me and Mitch turned to see what had caught his attention: it was the flagpole on one of the war machines slowly tilting towards the earth.

Six men pulled a rope attached to the heavy, short arm. The rope ran through a series of pulleys, but they still strained against the weight. As the short arm moved forward, the long pole, and the sling, moved towards the ground. When it was horizontal, other men locked it into place, and the men pulling the rope ran from the front of the machine to the back. There, they grabbed a second rope, while others arranged the sling on the ground and stuffed a tar-covered bale of straw into the pocket.

Leland watched the strange operation as if he was watching someone peel a potato, but me and Mitch had to keep closing our mouths because our jaws kept dropping. And then it became even more jaw-droppingly strange.

One man gave a signal, and everything let loose. Two men released the locked arm, the other six men pulled the rope. The short arm swung swiftly down, and the long arm shot skyward. Because it was so much longer, the tip travelled at an amazing speed, and the sling whipped over the top of the pole with even greater speed, flinging the straw-bale into the air at an incredible velocity. In an instant it was just a dot in the air, black against the grey sky. It rose and flew and then descended towards the far side of the river, crashing into the enemy line as they scuttled out of the way.

Leland turned to us and saw our faces. "Just a bit of play to ease the boredom," he said. "In battle, of course, they would be on fire."

Of course.

Despite Leland's assertions, I knew it was more than play; they were testing the range of their weapons. I wondered why they didn't test the catapults, but I figured the ammunition for them was too precious. Straw was easy to come by; cannonball-sized rocks were not.

Sobered by the display, we trotted back to our tent, where Leland left us in the care of our pageboys, telling us he would return to bring us to dinner.

"But aren't we having our dinner here?" Mitch asked.

Leland shook his head. "No, you'll be dining with Mordred in his tent."

"What if we'd rather not?" I asked, which earned me a slit-eyed look from the dark-haired page.

Leland's expression didn't change. "You are honoured guests. You cannot refuse."

With that, he rode away, leaving Mitch and me staring after him while the dark-haired page smirked at us.

I leaned close to Mitch. "So much for not being prisoners."

Chapter 13

Mitch

Our pages—Walter and the one I had started calling Jeff because he refused to tell us his name—brought us new clothes so we could dress for dinner. They weren't as fine as the ones the knights had stolen for us in Horsham, but they were colourful. I had red pants, a forest green shirt and a blue jacket with fancy embroidering around the edges and the buttonholes.

Charlie was dressed about the same but with a different set of primary colours, and we each had a floppy hat with a big feather sticking out of it.

"I'm not sure about this," Charlie said after we finished dressing, "these clothes itch, and I look like a clown. Are you sure the pages aren't playing a joke on us?"

I looked at my own clothes. "No," I said, "I'm not."

There wasn't anything we could do about it, our other clothes had already been taken away to be cleaned, so we sat at our table inside the tent and waited.

Leland came for us with three other knights. They called us out of the tent, and we marched in formation—two knights ahead of us and two behind—to Mordred's tent. Men along the way stopped to watch this mini-spectacle (anything to interrupt the boredom), which was so embarrassing I was almost glad when we reached Mordred's tent.

Guards pulled the tent door aside for us and we saw a long table running up the centre of the big room. Mordred sat at the head in his fancy chair while knights, in similar outfits to ours, sat along the sides. A blood-red cloth covered the table, and torches lit the room.

When Mordred saw us, he lifted his chalice. "Our guests of honour." The knights rose as one, each holding a cup aloft, and I suddenly wished I was back in the camp being stared at by bored men sitting around their campfires.

We were seated at the head of the table, right next to Mordred. When we sat down, so did everyone else. Mordred, I noticed, was still wearing our cloak, and the Talisman.

"My good knights," Mordred said. The table went silent. All eyes turned to him. "God has favoured us with victory. The Guardians, the cloak, the Talisman, all the elements required to make ours the Eternal Kingdom, and I the Eternal King." He raised his chalice again. "To the greatest victory, the greatest army, the greatest king the world has ever seen."

The knights cheered a solitary "Hooray," and drank.

The food came after that—platters of breads, meat, poultry, fish, some vegetables, and a lot of wine. The men ate and talked and joked, and occasionally toasted us, and King Mordred, while Mordred sat on his fake throne and eyed them all.

The setting seemed civilized enough, but we ate by hacking off bits of meat, stabbing it with our knives and stuffing it in our mouths. I was surprised that Mordred allowed us so close to him while we had knives in our hands. I'd have thought he'd have given us plastic cutlery, or make someone else carve up our meal, but that would have suggested he was afraid of us. Besides, the guards standing on either side of him would have put a sword through our throats if we even thought about making a move towards him.

Mordred didn't eat, but he drank, sparingly, and watched his dinner guests closely. When a muffled conversation about the possible outcomes of the possible battle grew loud enough for us to hear, he set his chalice down and laid his hands on the table, resting them as near to us as he could, as if we were comrades and compatriots.

"My friends," he said, causing the table to go silent. "There is no need for conjecture. There will be no battle. My father knows ours is the best army the world has ever seen, and I the best commander that ever was. To fight us would be folly, and I am far superior to him, or anyone else in all of history. Am I not to be your Eternal King? The Guardians ..." he raised his hands to indicate us, "who have sworn their loyalty, will fulfil the prophecy revealed to me. A great world awaits you all. We merely have to grasp it, we will not have to fight for it."

Picking up his chalice, he held it out as if in a toast. The knights grabbed their cups and held them up, speaking in unison. "To the Eternal King."

Mordred's lips twitched into a frown, as if their lack of jubilation displeased him, but then his smile returned, and he drank from the chalice as a signal to allow the knights to drink to him.

"See," he said to us as the dinner conversation rose again, "all is as it should be. You will fulfil your destiny, and I mine."

I nodded and smiled, and eyed Charlie to make sure he did the same. It wouldn't do any good to antagonize Mordred. We needed to stay close to Mordred, not only to keep an eye on our cloak, but to see what he was up to.

I looked once again down the table and around the room, hoping to find an old, bearded man among the guests, servants or guards but, as usual, the old Druid was nowhere to be seen.

The meal wore on, with the men becoming more boisterous as the wine flowed. Mordred, though he appeared languid, remained alert, his eyes moving beneath half-closed lids as he studied the men and listened to their conversations, made louder through alcohol.

I wondered why he wasn't getting drunk, then noticed that he was being served from a separate bottle kept especially for him. The drink in his chalice looked like wine, but I guessed it was mostly water.

When we were at last released, a squad of knights, accompanied by squires holding torches, marched us back to our tent.

We found Walter and Jeff sleeping by the glowing embers in the fire pit. We tried to get them to come inside but they refused, so we brought blankets and pillows out for them, which Jeff accepted grudgingly.

Our guards watched us without comment, but they

stood close, ready to stop us if we tried to stray too far from the fire, so we left the pages and returned to the relative warmth of our prison.

Chapter 14

Charlie

Our days fell into a routine that pretty much matched our first day. The pageboys made our breakfast and served it to us at our table. (As the days passed, they softened towards us, but I still checked the food before eating.) After breakfast, we would tour the front lines with Leland. Then we'd have lunch and, in the afternoon, he'd take us for a ride around the camp.

That was the most enjoyable part of the day. The camp was huge, and he took us to a different place each day, which kept us from getting bored. He even gave us some sword fighting lessons, though I think he did that just so he could handle our swords, which were bigger—but more bulky and harder to swing— than his own. He openly admired them, and called them battle-swords, and showed us how to use them.

Because they were so heavy, you couldn't fight with them the ordinary way, you had to use their weight to your advantage. Leland showed us how to swing the swords in a sort of figure-8 that, after a few awkward sweeps, seemed to make the sword light as a feather. Swinging the sword around like that, he told us, meant no one could get near you, and when the sword gathered maximum speed and momentum, it would slice through chain mail, and even light armour.

Relaxing as the days were, we continued to be on edge, looking out for the old Druid, straining to overhear conversations, and watching for signs of the coming battle. But we never found the Druid, we never heard anything helpful, and we saw no signs of increasing tension between the armies, until an overcast morning about ten days after we arrived.

We were, as usual, checking the front line with Sir Leland, when Arthur's troops catapulted a rock the size of a cantaloupe at the forward lookouts. It was unusual for them to be testing a catapult, but it wasn't out of the ordinary for the men to be shot at. As before, there was a warning shout, and the men scattered, and the rock harmlessly hit the earth. But then it bounced, hit the earth again, and bounced a second time. By now, it was slowing down, so one of the lookouts ran towards it to try and catch it. His companions shouted for him to stop, but he seemed to think it was a game, and he jumped in front of the rock as it dipped towards the ground again, holding out his hands to grab it.

The rock knocked him down and crushed his chest. Leland raced his horse towards the stricken man, and we followed.

By the time we got there, it was clear there was nothing we could do. The rock had caved his chest in, leaving a gaping crater of red, with white bones sticking out of it. Blood flowed, soaking his tunic and the ground around him. His face, white and lifeless, was frozen in an expression of surprise.

The man's companions gathered around him,

wailing, and shouting curses, and swearing revenge. We looked to the line of weapons and saw the upright poles of several of the war machines going down, and men with torches approaching the piles of tar-soaked straw.

"Sir Leland," I called, "they're going to start a battle."

Leland, who was bending over the dead man, looked up in alarm. He jumped on his horse and galloped towards the nearest war machine. Mitch and I took a last look at the dead man, realized there was nothing we could do, and followed Leland. By the time we caught up with him, other squads were cranking back the arms of the catapults.

"Stand down your weapons," Leland shouted.

The men stopped. Then the knight in charge of the nearest war machine ordered his men to continue. "They ask for war," he shouted to Leland, "we will give them war."

"They ask for nothing of the kind," Leland said. He swung his arm towards Arthur's army, and the crowd growing around the dead man. "You play a dangerous game. That man was not struck down by the enemy. He ran towards the missile, with the foolish intention of catching it. His death is no one's fault but his own." He looked at the war machine, the throwing arm now locked into place. "If you allow this incident to escalate, you will undo the work of King Mordred."

At the name of Mordred, the team manning the war machine stopped. Even the knight, who was standing in front of it, dressed in chainmail and helmet, with a sword in his hand, seemed to deflate.

"In the name of the King," Leland continued, "I order you to stand down."

Instead of putting a cap on it, this seemed to re-energize the knight. "For how long?" He swung his arm out, encouraging us to look down the line of weapons and lookouts. "How long do these men, these fighting men, have to stand here, impotent, with the enemy in their sight, and do nothing? Even now, with one of our members slain by the enemy, you bid us do nothing. Are you a knight, Sir Leland? Are you a man?"

If the insult stung Leland, he didn't show it. "King Mordred is wise beyond our understanding. War will gain nothing but death for us all. His plans are nearing completion. The enemy will be ours, victory will be ours, very soon, without another man falling." He stopped and looked at the knight, the men on the war machine, and then up the line. "Do you seek to undo the good done by King Mordred? Do you seek to thwart his will?"

At this, all the men, the knight included, looked at the ground. Leland stayed where he was, sitting tall in his saddle, moving his gaze from one group of men to the other. Everything hinged on them believing he carried an authority he didn't have, and I felt a cold hand squeeze my stomach when I realized he was the only thing standing between us and open warfare. Seconds ticked by, then the men with the torches turned away from the tarred hay bales, and the empty arms of the war machines rose slowly into the air.

"I admire your courage," Leland said, addressing a growing crowd, "and your loyalty to the King."

On cue, the crowd responded, "To the king," but

the words came out flat. I looked around at the men and knights, and not all of them looked pleased. Then Leland spoke again, in a voice that reminded me of Queen Elizabeth when she addressed her army at Tilbury.

"Be of good cheer, for victory is close at hand. King Mordred has the loyalty of the Guardians." He waved a hand in our direction. "And he wears the cloak, and the Talisman. Together, they will usher in the Eternal Kingdom, and King Mordred, with his loyal followers, will rule over all."

This time the cheer was energetic and heartfelt. Hats flew into the air and sporadic applause broke out. Leland smiled and waved, but I could see he was still troubled. He turned to us, his face grave. "We return now. Follow."

He galloped away and we struggled to keep up, riding straight across the field and through the camp, scattering startled men and boys. Shouts and curses rang out, but Leland ignored them. We galloped into the clearing in front of Mordred's tent, alarming the guards and drawing the attention of nearby knights. Leland jumped from his saddle, leaving pages to scramble after his horse.

"I must see the king," he said, striding towards the guards, who crossed their lances in front of the entrance. "It is of utmost importance."

"King Mordred is in conference," one of the guards said, not even looking at Leland.

"I bring news of trouble that could put us all in danger. Believe me, he will want to hear my report."

"The King is giving audience to an important messenger, he is not to be disturbed."

"He will want to be disturbed," Leland said, his voice rising.

The guards, at last looked at Leland, but held their ground. Leland stared back and, after a few tense moments, they stepped aside.

"Be it on your head." one of them said.

"As you wish," Leland answered. Then he looked over his shoulder at us and the gathering knights. "One of you will need to accompany the Guardians. Do not let them out of your sight." He didn't wait for an answer. The door flaps opened, and closed, and he was gone, leaving us with a dozen burly knights staring at us.

After a few moments of awkward silence, several knights stepped forward. Then a voice called from behind the group, "I will tend to them," and a man pushed into the clearing. I allowed myself to hope it might be the Druid, but it was just a regular knight, wearing a dusty tunic and a sword on his belt.

"By whose authority?" the guards asked.

"By whose authority do they claim the honour?" the man said, pointing at the three knights who had decided they wanted to be our babysitters. The knights turned to him and formed a short wall between him and us.

"By our authority," the largest of them said, taking a step forward, one hand on his hip, the other on the hilt of his sword.

The man didn't challenge him, Instead, he rushed to the side of the clearing and snatched the reins of Leland's horse from the page. Leaping into the saddle, he spurred the horse straight towards us. The three men scattered. As he rode past, he shouted, "Follow."

I looked at Mitch, who seemed uncertain. Then I looked at the knights, scrambling to regroup. It was clear they were coming for us. I pulled the reins and chased after the knight, with Mitch right behind.

Once away from Mordred's camp, the man eased his horse into a trot, and we followed him on the now-familiar path between Mordred's tent and our own. At our campsite, the man dismounted, so we did too. The man ordered our pages to hold the horses.

Walter took the reins from us, but the one we called Jeff stood with his arms folded over his chest. "Who commands it?"

"I do," the man said.

"And who are you?"

"By the grace of God, a knight. And by law, you are my servant." He held out the reins, but Jeff didn't move.

"Where is Sir Leland?"

"In conference with King Mordred."

Jeff looked at us through narrowed eyes, then back at the man. He shook his head. "This I must see for myself before I take your orders."

Then he ran off in the direction of Mordred's tent.

I thought the man would go mental at being disobeyed, but he just handed the reins to Walter and ushered us towards our tent. He nearly pushed us through the door, then followed.

"Your swords," he said. "Put them on."

"What?" Mitch said. "Why?"

"We haven't much time," he said. "Hurry."

Though we had been treated well all week, it didn't fool us. This could be a trick to find out if we were really loyal to Mordred. A wrong answer could get us killed.

I finished strapping my sword on but didn't move towards the door. "What do you want?"

"To take you to Arthur."

I felt my face go white.

"But we ..." Mitch said. I knew what he was thinking. In Mordred's camp, we might be in danger, but we were close to our cloak.

I still wasn't sure about the knight, but he looked trustworthy, and in a big hurry.

"What good will going to Arthur do," I asked. "Mordred has the Talisman, and our cloak. We need to stay near him to get them back."

The knight shook his head. "Mordred can do nothing without you. There are urgent plans afoot. I fear he is up to something, but when he finds you gone, he will have to change his plans."

"But he might attack," Mitch said.

"He won't dare," the knight said. "He needs to settle this peacefully, or he won't have a kingdom to rule. Now come."

Still, I didn't move. "But we're just Plan B. Mordred has accepted us as a sort of consolation prize. He's after our friend, Pendragon. He seems to think he is the real key. He sent Fergus to capture him, and he may return at any time, with Pendragon as his prisoner. That will give Mordred back any advantage he might lose if we get away."

At this, the knight smiled. "Fergus will not capture

Pendragon."

"How can you be so sure?"

The knight looked at me. "Because I am Pendragon."

Chapter 15

Mitch

As soon as he said it, it became so obvious that I couldn't believe I had missed it. Twenty years had passed, but I could see, just beneath the weather-beaten skin, the boy with the round face and red hair we had met on our first adventure.

"Pendragon? What are you doing here?"

He laughed. "Hiding from Mordred, of course"

"But that's …" Charlie said, "what are you … why …?"

"What's really going on here?" I asked, to stop Charlie from sputtering.

"Merlin is trying to keep Arthur king," Pendragon said, "Mordred wants Arthur to make him king, and Arthur wants to reunite his divided kingdom." He paused for a moment. "And I want to stop a war. There are over ten thousand men camped here and across the river, poised to kill each other. These green and peaceful plains may soon be red with blood, and buried beneath the bodies of dead and dying men, all because of the vanity of a single man."

I nodded. "Mordred."

Pendragon rubbed his stubbled chin. "I suppose that depends on where you stand. Mordred wants to be king, and he's willing to walk over bodies to fulfil his wish. Arthur wants his kingdom, all of it, and he doesn't care who he has to kill to regain it. This peace we enjoy is tenuous, held in place by a single thread, and Merlin is the one holding it."

"But what—" Charlie asked.

Pendragon cut him off. "No time. We leave now."

We went back to our horses and took them from Walter. "Where are you going?" he asked.

Pendragon mounted. We followed his lead. "On a tour of the camp," Pendragon said.

"With your swords?"

Pendragon shrugged. "I thought these young men could use a little sword practice."

He didn't wait for a response. He pulled the reins and trotted away, and we followed.

We went at a walk, meandering through the camp, occasionally waving at men we had become familiar with.

"A galloping horse means trouble," Pendragon said. "So, when there's trouble, we walk."

"What does a wizard have to do with all this?" Charlie asked when we were far enough away from anyone to overhear us.

Pendragon slowed his horse so we were in a tight line next to one another.

"Arthur wants to attack. He is getting old, but he is still hot-headed. Mordred was supposed to mind the kingdom while Arthur was in France, not take it over, and Arthur would love to see Mordred's head on a spike. But Merlin is appealing to Arthur, trying to get him to look to the future, to coming generations. He is afraid that, if the armies clash, Arthur will die, and he is convinced that, above all else, this must not happen. He has a notion that Arthur is to be the Eternal King, and it is only the promise of this that has kept Arthur in check."

"That's what Mordred wants too," Charlie said.

"Yes, that's why he's treating us so well," I added. "He wants to be the Eternal King, and he seems to think we can help him achieve that. I think that's the only reason he hasn't killed us. He has the Talisman, and our cloak, and he believes we can perform some sort of ritual for him."

"The Talisman is at the centre of this conflict," Pendragon said. "Who possesses it, who owns it, who it speaks to, and what it tells them."

"Mordred has it," I said, "but it's not his, so he can't have us perform the ceremony."

"And he hasn't told us what the ceremony is," Charlie said. "I'm not sure he knows himself."

"Exactly," Pendragon said. "Mordred assumes, because you are the Guardians, that you know what to do."

"Well, we don't," I said.

We were getting close to the edge of the camp now. Pendragon stopped his horse, and we did the same.

"And if Mordred discovers that, it won't go well for you," he said. "It is as you surmise, it's the only thing keeping you alive. That's why I must get you out."

I looked at him. He was staring ahead of us, at the

guards surrounding the perimeter of the camp.

"What's going to happen?" I asked.

He lowered his gaze. "We can't know. To stave off war, Merlin has sent Arthur a dream of what this battle would be like. It has convinced Arthur that he should talk with Mordred, but I don't know if that will do any good. Mordred has been resisting, but something is happening now. I think it will not be long before Mordred accepts his offers to attend the peace conference."

Charlie looked at him. "Well, that's a good thing, right?"

Pendragon shook his head. "It all comes back to the Talisman. Mordred will never give it up, and Arthur will never give Mordred the right to claim it. If they continue to remain stubborn, the only way to get what they want is to chance an horrific battle in the hope that they will survive and be able to claim the Talisman. Neither of them wants this, because they know, in the end, even if they win, they will rule over an empty kingdom."

"Stalemate," I said.

"Yes," Pendragon said. "I see no way out of this, and with two armies poised to strike at one another, sooner or later, by accident or design, a battle will start."

I thought of the incident we had just witnessed. Pendragon was right, someone needed to find a way to end the stand-off before someone like Leland wasn't around to keep the armies from clashing.

"You are the key to that," Charlie said.

Pendragon looked startled. "What do you mean?"

"Mordred wants you, very badly."

"Yes, but only because he thinks I'm one of the Guardians. I may very well be, but I know no more than you do about this ceremony he wants performed."

"That's true," I said. A sudden recollection made me gasp. "But he wants you for some other reason. That's why he's still seeking you." Pendragon and Charlie turned towards me. "Don't you remember," I said to Charlie, "when we first arrived. Mordred was so angry with Fergus for coming back without Pendragon that he sent him back to Sussex."

Charlie nodded. "Yes, but he knows—"

"He won't find me," Pendragon cut in, suddenly concerned. "What is it he wants Fergus to do?"

"He's going to bring in Aisley, and anyone his spies see her with."

Pendragon went pale. "If that is so, Ennora and Melvyn will be in danger."

"Ennora, and who?" I asked.

"Melvyn, my son, and Ennora, my wife. But what could he possibly gain by taking them prisoner?"

"I don't know," I said, "but he seems to think you, and by extension them, will give him an advantage."

Pendragon put his hand on the hilt of his sword. He looked back at the camp, then ahead of us at the open green land and drew a breath.

"We must leave," he said. "Now. We must send knights, and ride to rescue them before Fergus brings them here. If we can find him, if we can bring them, and you, to Arthur's camp, Mordred will lose his advantage."

Pendragon walked his horse forward. "Stay close," he said. We weren't at the front line with the catapults and war machines. Here, there were single guards, spaced widely. We aimed at a gap between them. "Move slowly. At my signal, we gallop as fast as we can. We'll have to outrun any pursuers and circle around to cross the river to get to Arthur's camp."

But before we could make our move, the sound of trumpets split the air, and a roar rose from the centre of the camp.

Pendragon stood in his stirrups and turned towards the camp. Riders were already coming our way. A group of three knights, with Leland in front, thundered between the tents, and entered the open field.

"We are too late," Pendragon said, his voice heavy.

"Guardians. Come," Leland shouted. "Arthur has agreed to talk. We parley for peace. Mordred requires your presence."

Chapter 16

Charlie

We were that close to getting away, and who knows what would have changed if we had. Mordred, seeing his advantage evaporate, may have attacked in anger, but he may also have agreed to a compromise. Whatever might have happened, it couldn't have been worse than what did happen.

As it was, we stayed where we were so as to not give away the fact that we were trying to escape. Leland and the knights pulled their horses to a halt as they reached us.

"Arthur is meeting with King Mordred on the field," Leland said. "You must be there. Hurry, the meeting begins presently."

He turned and galloped away, and so did we, with Pendragon following. Leland rode in front with the other knights surrounding us, all of them in battle dress—heavy chain mail, armour, helmets—and clutching broadswords or lances. As we galloped through the camp, knights ran in every direction, shouting to their squires and pages, urging them to fetch weapons, and help dress them for battle.

"A parley with the enemy is imminent," the mounted knights with us shouted, when we came upon groups of knights who were not sufficiently industrious. "Be prepared for treachery."

Those ready, rode their horses, following us, while those on foot surged forward.

I tried to hold my sword steady while the horse galloped, to keep it from banging into my leg, and the horse's flank, which made her run even faster. It was awkward, and painful, and staying on the horse was difficult. I gripped the reins with one hand the sword with the other and strained to keep up with Mitch and the knights. I could see he was struggling too, and I wondered what would happen if we fell. I wasn't sure, but I knew it wouldn't be good.

At last we reached the far side of the camp, where the line of men and weapons faced the river, and Arthur's army. Men primed the catapults with rocks. The knight, who Leland had recently told to stand down, was ordering his men to lock the arm of the war machine into position. Men with flaming torches stood near piles of tar-soaked straw bales, and behind them the army, rushing from the camp, assembled.

We rode past the line, into the open field. In front of us, Arthur's army was massing on the far side of the narrow river, a long line of horses and men bristling with swords, spears, and lances.

Crossing the river, and coming our way, were two riders. As they made the near bank, they galloped towards us. I assumed them to be Arthur and Merlin, because one was dressed in a flowing blue cloak, and the other had a long beard and a grey robe, both of which fluttered behind them. Arthur wore armour, with the cloak over top of it, fastened at his throat with a gold clasp like the one Mordred wore. But Arthur's was empty. Merlin had no armour or weapons, and carried only a long wooden staff.

Our company stopped near a group of mounted men already in the field. Mordred was in front, a small crown on his head, and our cloak covering his armour. His back was to us, but I was sure the Talisman would be with him.

He was flanked by his guards, all in armour, wearing swords and carrying long lances.

As we came up behind, Mordred glanced our way and smiled. Then he looked towards the east, where a small group of horses was galloping in our direction.

Pendragon came up next to us, also looking to the east. "Bad news comes this way."

His eyes stayed on the approaching figures, even as Arthur and Merlin stopped a few yards in front of Mordred.

Arthur, his long red hair flecked with grey, nodded towards Mordred. "My son," he said.

Mordred dipped his head slightly, "My father," he returned. "Arthur, the legendary king, but not my king."

"Neither are you king, Mordred," Merlin said. "You wear a crown, but it is hollow."

Mordred kept his eyes on Arthur. "Tell your conjurer to keep silent. We have no need of his tricks here." He swept his arm, "See before you a mighty army. Any treachery and they will swarm upon you."

"The same for you, my son," Arthur said. "It saddens me, but my good knights watch, as well, and if they see a sword raised in anger, they will strike."

Mordred let out a short laugh. "We agree we do not trust each other. That is a good way to start a negotiation."

"Start the bidding, then," Arthur said. "What will it take to buy peace?"

"I require nothing," Mordred said, touching the collar of our cloak. "I have the Talisman, the cloak and the Guardians." He turned to look at us, and the knights urged us forward. Pendragon held back, still watching.

"Then there is nothing to negotiate," Merlin said.

"I told you to keep your wizard out of this," Mordred said, addressing Arthur. "I do not trust him. I want him gone."

Arthur shook his head. "Merlin is a wise counsellor. Had it not been for his wisdom, his restraint, and his compassion, many of us would be dead already."

I had seen many things on our journeys, but nothing as amazing as this. Merlin, the famous magician from Arthur's court. I remembered reading about him. I looked again at him now that we were closer. His hair and beard were long, grey, and full, leaving little of his face exposed, but I could still make out a scar running up his right cheek, and curving around his eye in the shape of a question mark. As I looked, he turned my way, and I saw his eyes, blue, deep, and penetrating. I leaned over and nudged Mitch to tell him, but he was already looking.

"It's Mr. Merwyn," he said.

"It's Mendel," I said.

"Malcolm."

"Meryn."

"The Druid," he whispered.

Merlin nodded his head in our direction, then turned away and fixed his gaze on Mordred.

"If you have all you need, then why do you hesitate? Take the Guardians, and their cloak, to the Temple. Enter the chamber. Put the Talisman in its rightful place. You do not need an army for that, and we will not hinder you. There is no need for war."

Arthur moved his horse a step closer. "Send your army home, and we will do likewise. I will stand my army down this moment in return for your pledge to not attack. We can all go home, and you can go on your way."

Mordred sat upright in his saddle, his hands gripping the reins so tight his knuckles were white. Merlin raised his staff and pointed it at Mordred. "You wait because you know you do not have the right. You call yourself king, but you know Arthur is the true king. And you know that what you possess, because it is not yours, does you no good."

"Then that is my price," Mordred said. "My father will hand the kingdom to me. Now."

Arthur shook his head. "Impatience," he said, looking at the ground. "I had hoped manhood would have cured you of it. I had hoped holding my kingdom for me during my absence would allow you to see that power is worth waiting for." He raised his head and looked at Mordred. "But I fear all it did was fan the flames of your ambition. You must return the Talisman, and release the Guardians, with their cloak. I will not, I cannot, grant you the rights to the kingdom, or the Talisman."

"And I cannot allow you to have it," Mordred said. "You are old, and weak, and—"

"You cannot possess what is not yours," Merlin said. "The prophecy cannot be altered."

"The prophecy," Mordred said, "what do you know of prophecy. I hold the Talisman. It chooses to communicate with me. I know the truth. I have seen the future. I am to be Eternal King."

"Then keep the Talisman," Merlin said, "and retire your army. We will do the same. In the fullness of time, we will meet again, with sanguine hearts and cooler heads. War will gain nothing."

"I told you I am tired of your tricks, Merlin," Mordred said. "I will have what I ask."

"And when you do not get it, what will you do then?" Merlin asked. "You will not attack your father any more than your father will attack you. A war would be madness. Even if you found yourself king, there would be no kingdom left to rule."

Mordred leaned back in his saddle and stroked his sparse beard. "If both wish to avoid a fight, then one of us must yield to the other." He looked towards the riders again. "And soon, Arthur will yield to me."

The riders were close now, and the knights in both lines watched them closely. It might be a trick, a double-cross, a surprise attack. Even Merlin was gazing towards them, his brow lined with concern. Everyone in both armies seemed to be holding their breath. The field went silent, save for the clopping of horse hooves.

In the lead was Fergus, urging his flagging horse forward. Behind him rode one of his knights. Behind the knight, tethered by a rope, another horse carried a woman with dishevelled grey hair. Next to her a second knight led a horse ridden by a younger woman holding a boy in the saddle in front of her. All the horses were spattered with mud and breathing hard. I didn't recognize the young woman or the boy, but I assumed they were Ennora and Melvyn. The older woman was Aisley.

I took a quick look over my shoulder. Pendragon's face was white, his jaw clenched.

"Your Majesty," Fergus called to Mordred as he pulled his horse to a stop in front of us. "I return, with the prisoners, as you requested."

Fergus slumped in his saddle, as did the other knights. The horses stood with their heads down, foam dripping from their mouths.

"What is this?" Arthur demanded.

Mordred looked at his prisoners, his lips stretched into a grin. "My advantage," he said. "Unless you hand the kingdom to me. I will slay the captives."

From behind, I heard Pendragon draw a breath.

"You have gone mad," Arthur said. "There is no honour in killing innocents, and no incentive for me to yield. Three deaths, though regrettable, pale next to the thousands who would fall in a fight."

Arther looked angry, and disgusted, but Merlin seemed alarmed.

"These are no ordinary innocents," Mordred said. "What you see before you is your legacy. The old woman is your daughter. She had a son, Pendragon, your grandson. The others are his wife and child."

Arthur sat, stunned. He gaped at Mordred. "You talk madness—"

"Ask your wizard," Mordred said, pointing at Merlin. "He knows all about it. The maid,

99

Gwendolyn, you took to your bed. She had a woman child, who Merlin secreted away, just as he did to you. These are your kin, your legacy, and I will snuff it out unless you yield. My only regret is that your grandson proved to be a coward, and he remains out of my reach, hiding in the countryside."

From the back of our small company came a shout. "I am Pendragon. Release your prisoners and I will offer myself."

Calmly, Pendragon walked his horse forward. He edged between Leland and us and leaned over. "Be ready," he said.

I glanced at him. His jaw was set, his eyes bright. "For what?"

"An advantage."

He moved on, coming to a stop next to the horse carrying Ennora and Melvyn. "Let them go."

Mordred shook his head. "I fear I cannot do that. Your son carries your name, and therefore that of Arthur."

"My wife, and mother."

Mordred grinned. "Let's just say I like to keep things in the family, nephew."

He looked at Arthur, who was now looking sadly at the ground. "What is it to be, father? Your kingdom, or your legacy?"

Merlin turned to Arthur. "Mordred cannot, at all costs, become Eternal King."

Arthur put a hand over his face. I think he might have been crying.

"Yet the safety of Pendragon, and his family, is

paramount," Merlin continued. "They cannot be allowed to die."

"You are insane," Arthur shouted, looking up again. "This is not how negotiations are played, this is not how kings, or knights, or even common rogues behave. Be a man. Stand down and release the prisoners."

Mordred shook his head. Then two of his knights walked their horses towards Aisley and Pendragon, drawing their swords as they approached.

Arthur looked down again. Merlin looked our way, seemingly trying to communicate with us, but all I got was regret and sadness. Arthur drew a breath and looked at Mordred.

"Treachery and villainy," he said, his voice now weary and tinged with sadness, "but you leave no way out. It would grieve me to give you my kingdom, but I cannot stand by and allow you to slay my daughter, my grandson, and his family. If your black heart is set so on ruling, then I must—"

"Sire, you cannot," Merlin said. "The prophecy."

"Damn the prophecy," Arthur said. "I must choose one, and losing something I do not yet possess will break my heart less than losing my kin."

Merlin drew a breath and sat straight and still. His eyes seemed to glow. "Then do as your heart tells you."

"Release the prisoners," Arthur said. "Give them over to my care and I shall—"

Merlin pointed his staff at me. My horse whinnied and reared. I grabbed the reins to keep from falling from the saddle. In the flattened grass at my horse's feet, that an instant ago had been empty, a great snake lay coiled, its head cocked to strike. Leland saw it, drew his sword, and raised it to strike. The metal blade glinted in the sun, and suddenly, the quiet plain erupted with the shouts of ten thousand men.

Behind us, the thunder of hooves, and the battle cries of knights, rose to a deafening roar. Men loaded flaming bales into the war machines and readied the catapults. Across the plain, Arthur's army splashed through the shallow river and surged our way, like a giant wall, bristling with swords and lances.

Out of the corner of my eye I saw Merlin raise his staff. I looked again at the ground. The snake was gone.

Leland, his face ashen, lowered his sword. "God in heaven," he said. "What have I done?"

Chapter 17

Mitch

"Treachery," Arthur cried, his sword high as he spurred his horse towards Mordred.

"Kill the hostages," Mordred shouted, turning away, and galloping towards his approaching army, with Fergus right behind.

Arthur continued to charge, his sword swinging over his head.

"Sire, to your knights," Merlin shouted, already galloping towards Pendragon and his family. "Save them," Merlin shouted, looking in our direction, "and yourselves."

We were surrounded by Mordred's men. Two knights were with Pendragon and his family, and Mordred's two guards were rushing towards them to carry out his orders. I didn't know if we were hostages or not, but I wasn't going to stick around to find out.

I kicked my horse and, as she leapt forward, I pulled my sword from its scabbard and tried to swing it. It was heavy and unwieldy, however, so I couldn't get a good swing going, which turned out to be a good thing, because Charlie was right beside me. He had his sword drawn as well and was having just as much trouble with it. He looked my way.

"What do we do?" I shouted, struggling to keep on my horse.

Charlie spied Mordred's guards rushing towards the hostages. "Help Pendragon," he said, already turning his horse towards them.

Mordred's guards were not yet upon them, but the knights who had led them in were, and both drew their swords. Pendragon drew his own sword and swung it, cutting the rope that tethered Aisley to the lead horse. Then he turned towards the knight, barrelling into him, pushing him away as their swords clashed.

I took a quick glance over my shoulder and then wished I hadn't. Our guards, after a few moments of indecision, were now riding after us, their swords high, with Leland in the lead.

"Mitch, ride," Charlie shouted, pointing his sword to where Pendragon was fending off both knights. Charlie galloped to cut off Mordred's guards, who were rushing in from the side with Merlin behind them.

I pushed my horse forward and managed to swing my sword high enough to cut the rope to Ennora and Melvyn's horse, just as I crashed into the two knights from behind. I nearly fell off my horse, but they barely lost their rhythm. One kept flailing at Pendragon while the other turned his horse around mine, pinning me between himself and his companion. I turned in my saddle, unable to lift my sword for being penned in. The knight raised his sword to strike.

Then his dusty travel cloak erupted in a fountain of blood as the sharp end of a sword thrust out of his stomach. I gaped at it, disbelieving, and a little sick. The knight opened his mouth as if to scream, but all he made was a strangled sound as blood gushed from his lips. His sword fell from his hand and, as he leaned towards me, the blade disappeared back inside him. Then he slid to the ground, revealing Leland, holding a bloodied sword in his hand.

"I have much to atone for," he said. "I hope that will help." Then he turned to the stunned knights behind him. "There is no honour in killing women and children," he shouted. "Join me on the battlefield."

He rode away, passing through them. Most turned and followed. Most. Two of them rode straight at me.

I rode towards them, swinging my sword as the knight came near. Our swords clanged and vibrated so violently I thought my shoulder would break. The knight continued past, and I ducked as his companion took his turn, his blade swishing over my head.

I turned my horse, and the ground rumbled as a shower of stones rained down on us. They crashed into Mordred's war machines and bowled men over like tenpins. They were followed by burning bales, as Arthur's artillery unleashed their payloads. They hit the ground, exploding into flame.

It happened so fast I couldn't take it all in. Everything slowed down. I pulled the reins of my horse, turning her towards the knight, but unable to stop my gaze from straying over the field. Mordred's army was close. Catapults, smashed by stones. Bloodied men lying around the wreckage. Blazing war machines, and men, their clothes on fire, running, screaming, among the flames and smoke.

I became aware that I was screaming. A cry from deep inside, not of horror, but defiance. Somehow, I had raised the heavy sword up, and was swinging it over my head as I galloped towards the knight who was urging his horse towards me, his sword slashing the air, his mouth open wide. I think he may have been screaming too. I hoped the long reach of my sword would discourage him from getting close enough to hit me. His shorter sword was lighter and easier to manoeuvre, and I wished, not for the first time, that Grandfather had sent us one of those instead.

Thud.

More rocks.

Whump.

Another exploding bale.

More screams. The thunder of the armies getting closer. The knight galloping straight at me. My sword swinging towards him in a downward arc. The swoosh of his blade as it swept past my face. My sword striking his shoulder, hitting his armour, and to my surprise as, instead of denting it and knocking him from his horse, it cut through.

In the moment our horses passed, my sword followed its arc, slicing his shoulder, cutting his chainmail, and snapping his ribs. I turned. His hand no longer held his sword. It flopped, empty, at the end of an arm that, with half of his torso, sagged away from the rest of his body. Blood spirted. His lungs, pink against the darker red, expanded and contracted as he continued to breathe.

I screamed again, this time in horror. The knight said nothing. He just stared, slack-jawed, at the pulsing blood, then fell backward off his horse and lay on the ground, his eyes fixed on the cloudy sky above him as his broken chest spurted blood into the air like a crimson fountain.

I heard a shout as his companion galloped towards me, his helmet down, his sword swinging over his head. I pulled my gaze away from the horror and shook all thought from my mind. The exhilaration returned, and I shouted again, and swung my sword as Leland had shown us, aware of the blood flying from the blade as it gained momentum. It grew lighter the faster it went, propelled by its own weight. All I had to do was turn my wrist slightly, and the sword obeyed.

I rode towards the knight, my mind buzzing. He tried to keep his distance, but I swung the sword wide and, as we passed, it sliced through his side. He fell to the ground, writhing and screaming in pain. I kept going.

I looked to the side. Charlie held Mordred's guards at bay. His sword swished through the air. They backed up, but separated, coming at him from both sides. The knight that had led Aisley's horse swung a short sword at Pendragon. Merlin galloped from behind, unseen, his staff held like a lance. He thrust it into the side of the knight, who wore no armour and had only a padded shirt. The blow knocked him from his horse. He landed on the ground, screaming and clutching his side. Pendragon turned to the closest guard to help Charlie.

I rushed towards the other guard, swinging my sword. He turned towards me. I swung. He pulled his horse back, out of range. The sword continued its arc without any resistance, unbalancing me. I fell from my horse and hit the ground, knocking the breath out of me. The knight raised his sword to finish me, but Charlie's sword crashed into his side. It dented his armour but didn't go through, and the guard forgot about me and lashed out at Charlie.

"Mitch, watch out," Charlie shouted, fending off another blow.

I thought he should be the one watching out, but then I saw what he meant. The knight Merlin had knocked from his horse was on his feet now, coming for me. I was only halfway to my feet when he swung his sword. I blocked it and got to my feet. He swung again. All I could do was back away. Now that my sword had lost momentum, it was nothing more than a heavy piece of metal again. And the knight knew it. He came at me again, and again and then I stumbled backward and lay on the ground.

The knight stood over me, ready to strike. I tried to roll away, or raise my sword to block the blow, but I was frozen in terror. Another blazing bale exploded somewhere nearby. Men shouted. Horses screamed. Hooves thundered. It all faded to the background in that instant. I wondered how much it would hurt. Then, suddenly, he had no head.

I blinked, unable to comprehend. The body stood for a moment, blood spouting, as the head landed on my chest. I screamed and batted it away and crawled backward as the body slumped to the ground. Behind where the knight had been standing was Aisley, with a sword in her hand.

Suddenly, everything came back into focus, the noise, the smoke, the trembling ground, the smell of blood. The armies were nearly upon us. Aisley grabbed my hand and pulled me to my feet.

"Run," she said.

Chapter 18

Charlie

Mitch was in trouble, but so was I. That's how it is in battle, you just can't stop what you're doing to help someone.

The knight Mitch had distracted came for me while the other drove me back, my horse instinctively moving away from danger. I held my sword up to ward off the blows, but he left me no opportunity to strike. Merlin came in from the side and whacked him in the helmet with his staff. It only slowed him down, but it was enough. Pendragon came in from the other side and rammed his sword into the knight's chest. It didn't pierce the chainmail, but it knocked him off his horse. He splayed out on the ground, his helmet bouncing off his head. His horse jumped away, giving me room to swing my sword. The other knight took a blow from Merlin's staff and turned towards him just as my sword crashed down on him, cutting through his armour, and nearly taking his arm off at the shoulder.

A blazing bale exploded not twenty feet away. My horse reared. I gripped the reins.

"Grab his horse," Merlin shouted.

Pendragon's horse reared too, and came down on the unhorsed knight, one hoof crushing the man's head.

The noise became deafening. I struggled to put my sword back in its scabbard, then I urged my horse forward and leaned over as far as I dared, grabbing the reins of the riderless horse.

Then Mitch was there, trying to help Aisley up.

"No," she said, and ran to her own horse.

"Those are tired," Merlin shouted. "We need fresh mounts."

Pendragon grabbed another horse and shouted for Ennora and Melvyn to get on it.

Aisley pulled at the saddle bag on her horse. Mitch chased down another and jumped on.

"Hurry," Merlin shouted.

Aisley ran back to the horse I held, carrying her bag.

Mordred's army was nearly upon us. Hay bombs and stones rained down on them. Flames erupted, horses screamed, men scattered, body parts flew into the air.

"Leave it," Pendragon shouted to Aisley, who merely shook her head.

Merlin swung his staff, pointing at the advancing wall of horses, lances, and shields that was Arthur's army. "Follow," he shouted, and galloped away, swinging the staff in front of him.

Pendragon smacked the rump of Ennora's horse. It shot forward with her gripping the reins in one hand and Melvyn with the other. "Ride," Pendragon shouted, galloping after them.

Mitch looked at me and Aisley. "Let's go."

"We'll be right behind," I shouted.

He galloped away. Aisley tied her bag to the horse's saddle. The thundering hooves of Mordred's army thrummed through the ground, and the roar of his knights sounded like a huge beast. I saw swords, shields, lances, the white, terrified eyes of the horses.

"Hurry," I screamed, fighting the urge to leave her behind.

She pulled the knot tight. I grabbed her arm and helped her jump onto the horse.

"Go, go, go."

She galloped after Mitch with me right behind, barely keeping ahead of Mordred's men. We pelted at full speed, running from one impenetrable wall straight into another. A rock thudded to the ground in front of me. I turned my horse as it bounced passed. I didn't want to think what would happen if a horse stumbled, or if someone fell. I also didn't want to think what was going to happen when the two walls met with us in the middle.

The wall came nearer. I caught a glimpse of Arthur, his sword held high, riding at the front of his army, heading towards Mordred, who was leading his own men forward in a suicide rush, both with blue cloaks flapping behind them.

Merlin swung his staff, his voice booming over the din. "Make way, in the name of Arthur."

Incredibly, they did. It may have been because they knew him and were following his orders, or that the sight of a bearded man in a grey cloak swinging a staff frightened them, but the lead knights moved to create a small hole for us. We went in single file, Merlin,

Ennora and Melvyn, Pendragon, Mitch, Aisley, and me.

We slowed almost immediately, as the riders behind the lead knights had not made way. Merlin shouted and swung his staff and pushed forward and now we were being bombarded by Mordred's artillery instead of friendly fire. Rocks thudded and bounce through the ranks, leaving bloodied men and horses behind. Blazing bales hit with a thump, sending sticky, burning straw everywhere, covering horses and men, and causing chaos as they ran in all directions. The scent of burning tar and searing flesh permeated the air.

Then a different sound rose above all others. A resounding clash and roar and shouts and screams, all in the same instant. The ground shuddered. A jolt reverberated through the throng of knights surrounding us, as the rushing army ground to a halt.

The knights behind the first wave surged forward. We fought through the mass of horses and men, pushing forward until we cleared the lines of mounted knights, and waded into the foot soldiers. They, too, parted to let us pass, making our progress easier. It also helped that the rocks and blazing bales became less frequent.

When we got to the river, men were still crossing, though they were now walking, wading into the shallow water, and slogging across. We urged our horses down the bank to the other side, the water never rising above their knees. Once across, we found open ground and galloped through the line of Arthur's catapults and war machines, many of which lay smashed and burning amid the motionless bodies scattered over the pock-marked plain.

More rocks and blazing bales crashed down. We pushed our horses harder, heading for the relative quiet beyond.

Though the bombardment stopped, the sound of the battle still reached us. We ignored it, letting the horses slow to a trot as we entered Arthur's camp. There, we stopped, safe for the moment.

It seemed to be a camp of boys. No one remained except the pages. The tents looked bare, the piles of armour, the weapons, the men, the horses, were all gone.

The pages rushed to greet us, anticipating news of victory, but when they saw us, their glee turned sombre, and they stood silent, watching us climb off our horses, not daring to come forward to help.

"Tend to our horses," Merlin ordered, "and bring food and drink."

We dismounted amid a cluster of empty tents, exhausted, staring at the ground as the pageboys came near, their eyes full of questions. But the only answer was the roar of battle.

Pendragon grabbed Ennora and enveloped her in a fierce hug. She was a slight woman, shorter and with fair hair. She cried and laughed and sobbed into his chest. Then Aisley joined in, wrapping her arms around them both. Melvyn, a lanky boy with his father's red hair, stood shyly by until Pendragon pulled him into the group embrace. All of them seemed to be talking at once. "How?" "When?" "Who?" And then the words would melt into sobs or joyous laughter.

We sat by a dying fire, next to Merlin. The pages brought us food and we ate. Soon, Pendragon, still hugging Ennora and Aisley, joined us. I noticed Melvyn, having lost his shyness, sitting among a group of pages, holding their rapt attention as he told them tales of the battle.

For a long time, no one said anything. After searching for the Druid for days, and then finding him, as Merlin, I could think of nothing to say. But maybe that was because there was nothing anyone could say. So, we sat and stared into the dying flames, and tried to block out the sounds of combat.

I looked at Merlin, but he didn't seem ready for conversation. I sighed and leaned towards Mitch.

"Our cloak," I said.

"Yeah," Mitch answered.

There was nothing else to say.

We finished our food and drank some beer, and, after a long silence, Mitch turned to Merlin and asked, "What are we going to do?"

Merlin stared at the glowing embers of the fire pit. "I know not." He looked sad, and worried. "I fear for the future."

I thought of our cloak, and the Talisman.

Merlin turned his head slowly, gazing at the distant battle, where flames and smoke and dust rose into the grey sky, along with shouts and cries and the clang of steel. "This was not supposed to be."

I remembered the snake. "Then why—"

"It was the only way," Merlin said. "Arthur is old. Reflecting on his life has made him sentimental. He was going to trade his kingdom to save his family.

And that could not be allowed to happen." He lifted his staff slowly and pointed it towards the battle. "What is happening on that field is a tragedy, but it pales to insignificance against the darkness I see with Mordred as Eternal King. We are at a crossroad. The prophecy could go either way. It must go Arthur's way."

Mitch clutched his head with his hands, as if Merlin's words were giving him a headache. "What are you talking about?"

Merlin placed his staff on the ground in front of him and sat erect, his legs crossed. "It was twenty summers ago when last we met."

My mind whirled. We had met him a year ago, or about fourteen hundred years in the future. Then I realized that Merlin, or Mr. Merwin, or whoever, wasn't a traveller, as we were. For all his mysticism and knowledge, he was more like a normal man. He could only go forward in time and couldn't remember meeting us in 1916, or 1851 or any other time except those that were already in the past. Or his past, at least. Then I stopped thinking about it because my own head began to hurt.

"Since that time," Merlin continued, "with the Talisman returned to Arthur, the High Priests of the Druids, along with priests from the new religion, have been constructing a temple inside the Isle of Avalon. It represents the union of the two religions, the joining of the Land and the Sky. Its power is unmatched, and its culmination will keep the Land safe."

Mitch dropped his hands and shook his head. "What's all this got to do with us?"

"The Temple is complete. Except for the final act, the placing of the Talisman into its receptacle within the Temple. This will complete the union. And he who is rightful king at that time will become Eternal King. Mordred knows this and will stop at nothing to make sure it is he who takes that throne."

"So why capture us?" I asked. "Why take Pendragon and his family hostage?"

I noticed that Pendragon had left his wife's side and was now listening to our conversation. Merlin looked at him and nodded as if he approved. "Mordred has the knowledge, but not the understanding. Arthur, as well, knows only that he stands to be Eternal King. No one, not even I, knows the full implications. But it must be Arthur, for his heart is pure and he will protect the Land. Mordred has a dark heart and will seek to benefit only Mordred.

"Mordred's lust for power makes him blind. He thought, by stealing the Talisman and your cloak, and holding you, the Guardians, prisoner, he could get what he wanted. Only a Guardian, with the cloak, can access the Sacred Temple, and only the hand of Arthur, or his kinsmen, can unite the Talisman with the altar. Mordred had all he needed to do that. All except the right to be King."

Merlin shook his head and stared again at the dying embers. "I had hoped we could outsmart Mordred. Trick him into waiting. He held all the pieces, but he didn't have the key. I thought that was his weakness, but I underestimated the depth of his black heart. And this is the result." He took a breath and looked up to the slate sky. "But all is not lost.

There is yet a chance."

I struggled to keep my mouth shut. I could see Mitch doing the same. We didn't want to know the answer. Merlin stood, leaning on his staff, looking towards the battle.

"We must save Arthur," he said, "and the Talisman, and the cloak."

Again, we said nothing.

"We must return to the battle."

Chapter 19

Mitch

A weariness like I had never known descended on me. I struggled to my feet. Charlie did the same. Our horses were still skittish, but they were rested and no longer panicked. I mounted mine, soothing her by stroking her mane.

"I'm coming with you," Pendragon said.

"No," Merlin said, mounting his own horse. "Stay and keep your family safe."

"They are safe enough here. You'll need my help."

Merlin considered for a moment. "Very well."

Pendragon got on his horse while Ennora cried. "By the grace of God, you escaped. Now you're going back."

Pendragon reached down and stroked her cheek, turning her face upward to look at him. "I came back once, I will again." Then he turned his horse towards the battle.

Merlin nodded and we set off. We didn't gallop. We were afraid our horses couldn't take it. So, instead, we cantered past the artillery, most of the machines smashed and burning and all of them deserted, as the soldiers manning them either lying around them dead or had left for the battle. We crossed the river, then resumed a fast trot, the noise becoming louder, the air more choked with smoke and the scent of blood.

The grass all around had been pounded flat, and where the battle began it turned red, and was covered in a thick layer of grey that had me confused for a moment. As we came nearer, we found that Arthur's forces had pushed Mordred back towards his camp, leaving the ground between us, and where the fighting now was, humped and slick with blood and bodies.

"We must leave the horses here," Merlin said.

We dismounted and looked around for some way to tether them. Then Merlin spotted a foot soldier, his face bloodied, his clothes torn, staggering our way. "You there," he called.

The man saw us and cringed. "I'm not deserting, I'm not deserting."

"Certainly not," Merlin said, "you are performing a critical task. Come, hold our horses."

The man shuffled our way. He gathered the reins and stood, facing his own camp.

"Do not move until we return," Merlin said. Then he gave the man his staff to hold in exchange for the man's sword, and we waded into the battlefield.

It was slow going, stepping over the bodies of men and horses, and trying not to slip on the blood-slicked grass. Some of the bodies groaned. Others reached out to us for help, but Merlin urged us forward, stopping only occasionally to sooth the thrashing horses. He calmed them, stroking their foreheads, whispering words of comfort until they laid still enough for him to slit their throats. "The men came here of their own free will," Merlin said, leading us deeper into the field, "the horses were not given a choice. It is they who deserve our pity."

The battle had entered its final phase. A few hundred men clashed not far from us, and all around smaller groups of bloodied and exhausted men—six, four, even single pairs—grappled until some or all of them fell.

In the other battles I'd been in, it had been easy to spot the enemy, but here, all the men looked the same. Some—mostly the more important knights— had red or black dragons emblazoned on their breastplates, but the other knights and foot soldiers looked, to me, identical. Fortunately, none of them came for us, friend, or foe. We must have looked intimidating, four men, well-armed and fresh to the fight, led by Arthur's legendary wizard. The dwindling number of men around us fought, killed, died, and kept their distance.

"Can Arthur still be alive?" I asked, gaping at the carnage.

"They live," Merlin said without slowing. "If Arthur or Mordred had been killed, the fighting would have stopped. They will be here, in the thick of battle."

Arthur's army had pushed Mordred's men through their own artillery line, near to the edge of their camp. The war machines now lay burning, and the tents on the edges of the camp were on fire. Fewer bodies littered the ground here, but the men still standing upright were doing their best to increase the number.

Off to the side, a group of six fought a frenzied skirmish. After a brief flurry of swords and a clash of shields, five men fell, leaving one wounded knight to trudge back towards the main battle. On the other side, one of Arthur's knights battled two of Mordred's men. In seconds, none of them were standing. If the battle didn't end soon, everyone on the field would be dead or dying. The overriding feeling wasn't panic, or fear, or even concern over our cloak, but sadness, and relief that no one was challenging us. Then I saw a group of four men coming our way. Modred's men.

We stopped and held our weapons ready. The group had shields and swords, and one carried a lance. When they saw us, they stopped. They watched us, their swords at their sides, their shields held low.

"Why are they not advancing?" Pendragon asked.

Then the men backed away, turned, and ran.

"They're afraid," Charlie said.

Merlin shook his head. "No, they carry news. Stay ready. We will have company soon enough."

The men were already out of sight, hidden among the confusion of fighting men, riderless horses, and fires. Then, from out of the smoke, a rider on a black horse cantered our way, a shield in one hand, a sword in the other. His armour, his helmet and his shield were black, polished to a high sheen, and at his throat, a circular black clasp held a blue cloak that billowed out behind him.

He stopped when he saw us and raised his visor. "So, the news is true," he said, shouting over the battle's roar. He swung his sword over his head, slicing through the air. "I could kill you all with a single blow. But I won't. I'll leave one of the Guardians to make me Eternal King and kill the rest of you."

He urged his horse forward, still swinging his sword.

"Spread out," Merlin said. "Give him more targets."

"Strike him from behind when he turns," Pendragon said. "Strike his horse if you must. We need him on the ground."

Panic drove away my sadness. I raised my sword, my mouth dry, my stomach cold.

Then another horse galloped from the gloom, a lance pointing our way, but he wasn't coming for us. His armour was dented and bloodied. A blue cloak fluttered behind him, making his armour shine in contrast. On his breastplate was the symbol of a red dragon.

Mordred bore down on Merlin, who stood ready, but Arthur called out and Mordred turned his horse. He pulled his visor down and galloped towards his father. Arthur drove his horse forward, the lance aimed at Mordred. Mordred raised his shield and swung his sword. The riders clashed. Arthur's lance smashed into Mordred's shield, driving him backward as he lashed out. Arthur dodged the blow. Their horses moved on, and both men fell to the ground.

"Arthur," Merlin shouted.

We rushed forward. Then the men stirred. Mordred clambered awkwardly upright, struggling against the weight of his armour. Gripping his sword, he shuffled towards Arthur, who was still on the ground.

Arthur struggled to rise. Mordred's shuffling steps became a trot. He was going to be upon Arthur before he could get to his feet, and we were still too far away to help. Mordred began a shambling run. He raised his sword. Arthur pushed himself off the ground until he was on his knees, but without a weapon. It was going to be over in seconds.

Mordred readied for his final lunge, then Arthur lifted the fallen lance. Mordred hit it full on, its point striking the joint in his armour at his midsection. His momentum carried him forward until our cloak billowed out behind him and I saw the bloodied tip of the spear protruding from his back.

We stopped, shocked and relieved. I sheathed my sword, glad that I hadn't needed to use it. Charlie did the same. But then I felt a growing unease. Mordred had not yet fallen.

Arthur braced himself, struggling to hold the lance as Mordred stayed on his feet and, incredibly, took a step forward.

"Surely he's dead," Pendragon said.

"Not yet," Merlin said. "Hurry."

We ran forward again. Mordred gripped the lance with his free hand and pulled, sliding closer to Arthur, leaving a trail of blood and gore as the lance seemed to grow out of his back. Arthur stared as if transfixed. Mordred, pressing and pulling with all his waning strength, took another step.

"Arthur," Merlin shouted, "look out."

But Arthur didn't move. Mordred swung his sword, catching Arthur on the side of his helmet with the tip. Both men fell again. This time, they didn't move.

Merlin threw his sword down so he could run

faster. "Save Arthur."

"Get the cloak," Charlie said, sprinting ahead of me.

Pendragon, his sword still in his hand, shouted, "Watch out, we have company."

A horse galloped towards us, but the rider had no weapon and wore no armour. His clothing was torn and bloody. He pulled his horse to a stop and jumped off, stumbling as he ran towards Mordred's body.

"It's Fergus," Charlie shouted. "He's after our cloak."

Chapter 20

Charlie

"Save the Talisman," Merlin shouted.

I ran faster, my sword bumping and clanging against my legs. Fergus ran too, straight for the cloak, and the Talisman. I didn't care about the Talisman; I wanted our cloak. If Fergus got it, we'd be trapped here forever.

Fergus lunged for the fallen Mordred. He grabbed the cloak and pulled, trying to run back to his horse, but the cloak was still attached to Mordred by the clasp holding the Talisman. Fergus grunted and pulled, dragging Mordred's body with him, opening the gap where the lance had pierced him, dumping more of his guts on the bloody ground. I dived over the guts, the lance and Mordred, landing on Fergus and grabbing our cloak.

We tumbled to the ground. The cloak tore away from Mordred's throat. I grabbed it and pulled, and Fergus kicked me in the side. The breath whooshed out of me. Fergus snatched the cloak and ran.

"The Talisman," Merlin shouted again. "Arthur needs it. Save it, at all cost."

I was up in an instant, gasping and limping. I tripped over my sword and fell again and wasted a precious second and a half by unclasping my belt and leaving the sword behind. This time, when I got to my feet, I ran and kept running. Fergus had a big lead, but I was faster.

He ran to his horse, trying to grab the reins as she shied away. He looked over his shoulder. I was nearly on him. He let the horse go and ran. And I ran faster.

We ran through groups of fighting men, jumping over corpses, and dodging rampaging horses. He was nimble, but tired. I came closer. He glanced back and changed course. Then my stomach went cold as I saw where he was heading.

A war machine lay on its side, splintered and blazing, and Fergus ran towards it. I chased after him, gaining, but he was almost at the fire. He brought his arm back, the one holding the cloak, preparing to throw it into the flames. The cloak fluttered out behind him. I dived for it.

I felt a tug as Fergus's throwing arm tried to swing forward and couldn't. The sudden stop unbalanced him. He fell. I scrambled backward, pulling the cloak with me. He grabbed the other end and pulled back and we lay there, in a prone tug-o-war, pulling and straining and struggling to get to our feet.

I got a foot under me and leaned back but Fergus did the same. His feet dug into the earth while mine slid over a slick of blood. Slowly, he pulled himself, the cloak, and me closer to the burning war-machine. I dug in and leaned further back, and the cloak slipped in my hands. I gripped the clasp that held the Talisman, struggling to stay upright, fighting the urge to let go so I could escape the searing heat. Fergus grunted and pulled, leaning so close to the blaze I thought his clothing would catch fire. If I could just hold on for a few more seconds, he'd have to let go. No one could stand that close to the flames for long.

Then the clasp came free as the pin attaching it to the cloak ripped through the collar. I fell back into the mud and blood. Fergus, still holding the cloak, fell into the fire.

"NOOOOOOOO!"

I jumped up. Fergus was writhing and screaming, with our cloak draped over him, already in flames. I tried to grab it, but I couldn't get past Fergus's thrashing legs. His clothing burned; his head looked like a back skull. A screaming black skull. Then the screams stopped. His skin crackled like a steak on a grill and, just before I turned away, his eyeballs exploded.

I sank to my knees, shaking my head. There were tears in my eyes and a hollowness in my chest. We were never going home. My mind froze. I couldn't think what to do next. Then a voice from behind helped me decide.

"Stand and face me or die on your knees."

I stood and turned. It was Sir Alwyn, his helmet gone, his hair in disarray, his eyes wide and white. He was panting, exhausted, each heaving breath sending a spray of saliva and blood through his clenched teeth. In his hand he held a sword, dripping with blood.

"The battle's over" I told him.

"Not ours," he said, raising his sword. "I still owe you for what you did to me back at that woman's hovel."

At that moment, it was all the same to me. Our cloak was gone. We were trapped. What was the sense of going on? I didn't move, I just stood, waiting, wondering if I would wake up in the bedroom, with Dad and Mom, both mad as hell, standing over me. Would it be that, or …

"Is that how you prove your courage," a voice called. I looked beyond Alwyn. It was Mitch, running forward, his sword swinging over his head. "Killing an unarmed man. How about a fair fight?"

Alwyn's bloody mouth pulled into a grin. He turned away from me and faced Mitch.

"Lay on," he shouted. "I'll kill you and then finish your snivelling brother."

Mitch came towards him, his sword arcing towards Alwyn's head. Alwyn's sword flashed. The clang of steel on steel rose above the roar of battle. Mitch's sword was knocked sideways, and Mitch with it. He swung again, but without much strength. Another clash and Mitch was driven backward.

"Not so clever now when you can't take me by surprise," Alwyn said, swinging his sword, driving Mitch further back. "You fight like a woman. You're no knight."

Mitch swung again, catching Alwyn off-guard. Even so, he blocked Mitch's blow and went on the attack again. Mitch couldn't win, and Alwyn was getting tired of playing with him. He raised his sword, ready for the kill. Then Mitch ran away.

"Coward," Alwyn shouted. "I knew you were a coward."

He went to run after him, but Mitch stopped a safe distance away. He lifted his sword, looked at me and shouted, "Break!"

Chapter 21

Mitch

I hoped Charlie would hear and remember. It was our code word. A way to double-team and escape an enemy, taught to us by Ellen in 1588.

Alwyn stood where he was, momentarily confused. I ran towards him, my sword held high. He prepared to meet me.

Charlie knew what I was doing. He ran forward, fast. I timed my approach, waiting for Alwyn to swing. As I got close, I drew my sword back. Alwyn raised his. Instead of clashing with him, I threw my sword, and he swung his to bat it out of the way. That was my chance. Before he could ready another strike, I leapt at him, crashing into his chest just as Charlie rolled into the back of his knees. He went over backward and landed with a grunt.

Our ploy had worked, but I think it hurt me more to land on his metal breast plate than it did him falling onto the ground. I was winded and struggled to stand. He pulled his sword back for another strike. I rolled off him but knew I couldn't get far enough away in time. Charlie jumped in front of me, landing on Alwyn's outstretched arm. I heard a sickening snap and Alwyn screamed and his hand opened, and the sword fell to the ground. I lunged for it. Alwyn grabbed for me with his good hand. I scrambled away and stood, gripping his sword.

"So now it's you killing an unarmed man," Alwyn said, still on the ground. I didn't answer him, I just swung the sword over my head and heaved it as far as I could. It spun in the air and landed in the fire Charlie had been standing by.

"Com'on," I said to Charlie, but he just stood there, holding the Talisman in its golden case.

"The cloak," he said.

"What—"

He gestured towards the fire.

"Gone."

I sucked in a breath. My head felt light. Then I shook it away. "We can't do anything about that now. Arthur needs us. Hurry."

We jumped away as Alwyn, again, tried to grab us with his good arm. Then he tried to get up, so I stomped on his ankle. It didn't break, but it brought out a satisfying yelp and I knew he wouldn't be able to chase us.

We ran back as fast as we could. Around us, the battling clusters slowly ceased as news spread through the field. The men, from either side, lowered their swords and gazed at the dead. They did not look victorious. Instead, they looked ashamed.

When we got to Arthur, Merlin and Pendragon had removed his armour and laid him out on the ground. Merlin knelt next to him, rubbing a mixture of herbs into a deep gash on the side of his head. Pendragon stood nearby, where Arthur's armour was piled, holding Arthur's cloak in his arms.

"The Talisman, quickly," Merlin said when he saw us. "Take it from its holder. Give it to Arthur."

Charlie fumbled at the clasp. It popped open and the Talisman fell out. I scooped it up and pressed it into Arthur's limp hand. Nothing happened for a moment, then his fingers closed around it. I let out a breath I hadn't known I was holding.

"We need to move him," Merlin said. "Get something to carry him on."

Pendragon, Charlie, and I ran to where a smashed catapult lay on its side. We struggled to pull the bottom free.

"It's lashed tight," Pendragon said. "We've got to cut through the ropes."

I went for my sword but realized I had lost it in the fight with Alwyn.

Charlie ran off and returned with his. "Use this."

He pulled the sword from its scabbard and handed it to Pendragon. We stood aside as he chopped and cut and heaved, and then we helped him pry the boards free, and we had a platform.

We dragged it to where Arthur lay. Merlin and Pendragon placed him on it, covered him with his cloak and laid his sword by his side. Then we gathered ropes and tied them to the boards and began sliding the pallet over the ground, back towards his camp.

The wood slipped easily over the slick grass, but going was slow because we had to keep stopping to move bodies out of the way. When others saw what we were doing, and who was on the pallet, they came and helped. Soon we had enough men to carry him and made better time.

At the edge of the battlefield, we found the man holding our horses, and Merlin's staff.

"I regret that I do not have your sword to exchange for my staff," Merlin told the man.

Charlie began unbuckling his belt.

"Here," he said, "you can take mine."

But the man put a hand on his shoulder to stop him. "No," he said, handing Merlin his staff, "the time for weapons is past."

He joined the men carrying the pallet with Arthur on it, and we rode the horses next to them. They walked slowly, but steadily, as if bearing a body to a funeral pyre. Except that Arthur was alive. We forded the river, the men holding Arthur high, out of the water, and approached the camp. There were many pages, but few men, and nearly all of them were seated around the rekindled fire, bandaged and bloody.

"Away, away," Merlin said, as men and pages crowded around Arthur. "Tend to yourselves and leave us to tend Arthur."

But one knight remained. He carried no sword and wore no helmet. Stains, red and wet, oozed from the tunic beneath his battered chainmail. Sweat plastered his black hair to his skull, and blood spatters covered his face. Merlin greeted him with an embrace. "Sir Bedivere," he said, "where are the others."

The knight called Bedivere stepped away and looked at the ground. "Dead."

Merlin looked at the men sitting and lying around the fire, and the others, now straggling into the camp.

"All?"

"Only I and Sir Lucan returned," Bedivere said, "and Sir Lucan has breathed his last."

Merlin seemed to deflate. If he hadn't been leaning on his staff, I think he might have collapsed. Ignoring him, Aisley and Ennora came to Arthur, cleaned his wound and bound a bandage around his head.

Pages and wounded men continued to crowd around, despite their efforts to disperse them. I recognized some as knights we had met in Mordred's camp. There were pages with them too, dusty, dirty and some of them bloodied. With their camp in ruins, they had nowhere else to go, yet no challenges came from Arthur's men, nor anger from either side. There were no victors, and no vanquished; there were only survivors.

Arthur lay still, his face ashen, the Talisman still clutched in his hand. Slowly, colour returned to his face. His grip on the Talisman tightened. He opened his eyes.

Those crowding around him gasped. Pages rushed away and in moments, pillows appeared. Aisley and Ennora propped his head up so he could see. He raised a hand, the one without the Talisman, and pointed with a shaky finger. "My loyal men," he said, his voice rasping. "Brave, loyal, and so few." He coughed. Aisley wiped blood from his chin. "Look to me no more. Find your pages, your squires. Tend your wounds, return to your homes. The war is done."

The crowd dispersed in silence, all but Bedivere, who knelt beside Arthur. "I remain with you, my liege.

Arthur gazed at him. "Sir Bedivere. Where are the others, my knights of the table?"

Bedivere bowed his head. "I am all that is left."

Arthur said nothing, but he looked away from Bedivere, hiding his face. When he turned back, his cheeks were wet. "All dead, for my sake. Had I lived, I would spend my days grieving their loss."

"But Sire, you do live," Bedivere said.

Arthur shook his head. "Not for long. And there is much to do. And you must do your part." He looked around, at me, Charlie, and Pendragon, and fixed his gaze on Merlin. "You know what to do."

Merlin nodded.

Arthur lifted his hand again, pointing in our direction. "And these men?"

"Mitch and Charlie," Merlin said. "They are the ones who saved you, who saved the Talisman, and who will save the Land."

"Closer," he said. We stepped forward as he tried to focus on us. Then his eyes widened. "It is you. The Guardians. You and your friend, Pendragon, returned the Talisman to me, many years past, when you were mere boys, and now you return it to me again."

I nodded. "We did." I paused, wondering if I should call him your Majesty, Sire, Liege or just Arthur, but he spoke before I could decide.

"You have aged little, yet I am an old man."

"We're travellers, sir," Charlie said, as if that explained everything.

He shifted his gaze to Pendragon. "And you? You were with them? A man now. Are you really my grandson?"

Pendragon cleared his throat and shuffled his feet. Merlin brought Aisley to stand at Pendragon's side. "Your daughter," he said, "and her son." He waved a hand towards a nearby campfire where Melvyn and some pages tended to the wounded. "And his son, accepted by your pages, and already learning to be a knight. Your legacy lives. And, thanks to their bravery, the prophecy can yet be fulfilled. But there is little time, and much to do."

Arthur slumped back on the pillows. "Then do what you must."

Merlin nodded and turned away, striding into the camp. "A cart," he commanded. "One that can travel fast. And horses. Quickly."

Arthur struggled to sit up. "Before I die, I must reward you. For your bravery, your loyalty, and your future deeds. Come." His hand dropped over the edge of the planks, his palm open, his finger curling, indicating that he wanted us near him. We walked to his side. "Kneel," he said. We did.

Then he lifted the sword lying next to him. Despite having been in battle, it gleamed, and the jewels decorating the hilt and scabbard twinkled. He laid the Talisman aside and drew the sword. It looked heavy, and Arthur was fading, but he held it as if it weighed nothing. He touched Pendragon's shoulder. "Pendragon, my grandson, loyal and brave." The sword lifted. Its gleaming blade floated towards me and tapped my shoulder. "Mitch, the cunning warrior." The blade rose over my head and moved to Charlie. "And Charlie, fearless in battle. Rise now, Sir Pendragon, Sir Mitch, and Sir Charlie."

We stood. Arthur laid back, the sword still in his hand, too exhausted to return it to its scabbard. Bedivere gently took it from him and sheathed it while I put the Talisman back in Arthur's hand.

A cart appeared, pushed and pulled by a group of boys and young men, and Melvyn. It was a rickety thing, with four wheels, flimsy, latticework sides and a small platform for a driver. Other boys came leading horses.

"Get Arthur onto the cart," Merlin said. "Someone will have to ride with him, to keep the Talisman from slipping out of his hand. The others will ride with me, fast to our destination. The day is coming to a close, we must move quickly."

"Where are we going?" Charlie asked.

Merlin didn't stop. He strode past him, to Arthur's side.

We lifted the board—Bedivere, Aisley, Ennora helping—with Arthur lying on it, and carefully slid it into the back of the cart. Blankets and more pillows arrived to keep Arthur warm and comfortable. Pendragon secured it with ropes, but I wondered if it would do any good.

Merlin mounted a horse and raised his staff into the air.

"Make haste," he said, looking at Bedivere. "Meet us on the shores of Avalon."

Chapter 22

Charlie

Ennora and I were chosen to ride in the back of the cart with Arthur, solely because we were among the smallest and lightest in the company. I was going to argue that Mitch actually weighed a little less than me, but Merlin seemed set on taking him, and leaving me with the cart.

I rode, kneeling in the side of the cart, next to Arthur, clasping his hands together with the Talisman between them, like a Talisman sandwich. Ennora sat in the front, just behind Bedivere, who perched on the driver's platform. The others rode off and were soon out of sight, even though Bedivere drove the cart like a madman.

We bumped and bounced, and I had to squeeze Arthur's hands tight to keep the Talisman in place. Ennora had the job of keeping Arthur's head still by cradling it on a pillow in her lap. It didn't look easy, and if she slipped, he'd certainly have been bashed unconscious, or worse, by the cart rattling over the uneven terrain. As for me, my knees were being pounded and my sword kept bouncing and smacking me in the side, but there was nothing I could do about that except steal a pillow or some blankets from Arthur, and I wasn't going to do that. I didn't want

Ennora to think I couldn't take it.

She was slight, but strong. She had, after all, ridden with her son, tearing headlong into an advancing army at a speed that nearly made me bounce out of my saddle. I wasn't about to do anything in front of her that made me look soft. She saw me looking at her and smiled. I felt myself blush and turned away.

"Did you truly know my husband when he was a child?" She had to raise her voice to be heard over the rumbling of the cart.

I nodded. "We were all the same age. About as old as Melvyn is now."

"And yet my husband is advanced in years, and you remain young men?"

"It's complicated."

"And what he tells me is true?" She looked down at Arthur. "You served the King even then?"

"Yeah, the three of us outsmarted Mordred, and Fergus, and we got the Talisman to the King." I looked at Arthur, who had looked so powerful back then, and so helpless now. "It was a long time ago."

"But you visited before? You will visit again?"

I looked at Arthur, and then at her. "Not for a long time."

She nodded and went silent, concentrating on Arthur. The bandage around his head was bloody but it wasn't fresh blood, so the cart ride wasn't hurting him. Much. He moaned occasionally and looked through the sides of the cart as Ennora stroked his head.

A few miles from the camp, the land became dotted with scrub brush and small trees and covered with a lush carpet of green. The cart bounced as Bedivere urged the horses forward, but the wheels made little more than a swishing sound through the tall grass, and the horse's hooves became muffled, so the most prominent sound was the creaking of the cart. Then the air became cooler, fresher, and still. But it was kinda spooky.

Then Arthur spoke. Ennora tried to listen but couldn't bend that far and still hold him steady, so I leaned over and put my ear close to his mouth. "We must stop."

I looked at him to be sure I had heard him right. He nodded once, his eyes bright and his expression anxious.

"Stop," I yelled to Bedivere.

Bedivere looked over his shoulder, uncertain.

"Now."

He brought the cart to a juddering halt. "What is it? Is Arthur in danger?"

"I don't know. But he wants us to stop."

Bedivere came to the side of the cart. "My Lord, time is short. We must be quick."

Ennora helped Arthur pull himself into a semi-sitting position. "There is time enough. And you have an important task to perform." He picked up the sword that was still at his side, the gleaming, jewelled sword he had knighted us with, and handed it to Bedivere. "There is a lake, not far beyond that stand of trees. Take the sword, throw it into the lake, and return."

Bedivere held the sword, staring at it in amazement. "But Sire, Excalibur? You cannot mean this."

"I do," Arthur said. "I cannot continue my journey until this task is complete. I am unable. The responsibility falls to you. I beg you, Sir Bedivere, do this final kindness for me. Do not fail your King."

Bedivere bowed and backed up a few steps, then he turned and headed for the cluster of trees Arthur had pointed out. I was glad Arthur had asked him to do it. It was creepy. Even with Ennora and Arthur there I felt uneasy, like I was in an old house where the wood creaked and moaned, and you had the feeling someone was watching, even though you knew (hoped) you were alone. I just wanted Bedivere to chuck the sword into the pond so we could could got out of there.

He disappeared into the trees and, a few minutes later, he came back without the sword.

"The deed is done," he said.

Arthur raised himself up on his elbows. "Tell me what you saw."

Bedivere hesitated, taken aback by the question. "I saw a splash, and ripples on the lake."

Arthur slumped onto the pillows. Ennora gripped him by the shoulders to keep him from sliding off her lap while I struggled to keep the Talisman clasped in his hands. "You are my loyal knight, Sir Bedivere, and I have charged you with a most important task. Return. Do as I ask. And do not pretend to deceive me."

Bedivere lowered his head. "Forgive me, Sire. It is an elegant sword. To condemn it to rust at the bottom of a muddy lake—"

"Go, Sir Bedivere," Arthur said, his voice heavy with sadness. "I beg you, do not return until the deed is done."

Bedivere headed for the trees again, walking more slowly this time. We watched him go.

"Follow," Arthur said. "See that he does it. He cannot fail again."

The last thing I wanted to do was head into that thicket, but I knew we weren't going to leave until Arthur believed the sword was at the bottom of the lake. I started after Bedivere, but my sword clanked and rattled as it bounced against my leg, so I took it off and laid the sword, in its scabbard with the belt wrapped around it, next to Arthur where Excalibur had been. As soon as Bedivere disappeared into the trees, I ran after him.

I hid among the bushes and saw him uncovering the sword. He had buried it under a pile of leaves at the base of a large tree, planning, I assumed, to return later and retrieve it. He picked it up and held it in front of him, admiring it. He wasn't keeping it out of greed, he was awed by the sword, and there was a sadness in his eyes. He stood for a while, mooning over it, then he sighed and bent down, preparing to return it to its hiding place. I stepped into the open where he could see me.

"So," he said, his voice betraying neither surprise nor guilt. He stood straight, cradling Excalibur in his arms, "Arthur has sent a spy to be certain I follow his orders." He sounded resigned, not angry. "Come, then," he said. "We shall commit this folly together."

Just beyond him was a lake. The surface of its crystal water mirrored the grey sky, and the shallows near its banks were thick with cattails and reeds. It looked peaceful, and inviting, but I again got the feeling of being watched.

"Then let's do this," I said, walking past him to the lake, "so we can get out of here."

I walked through waist-high grass, to a gap in the reeds that provided a clear view of the lake. Bedivere came up beside me, still holding Excalibur. He stood silent for a few moments, then said, "Thank you."

"For what?"

"For being here. To my shame, I would not have had the courage to follow my King's last command. This sword, it carries meaning, authority. It goes against every fibre of my being to do Arthur's bidding. I fear, in his grief, his mind has betrayed him. No man or King, with a peaceful mind, would command the destruction of such a beautiful sword."

But still, he hesitated. The lake, I felt, stared at me, willing us to give up the sword.

"Did you notice," I said, "that Arthur didn't command you? He could have said, 'As your King, I command you to follow my order,' but he didn't. He asked. He wants you to do him a favour. Of your own free will. But I suspect it's the most important favour you'll ever do for him."

Bedivere nodded. Slowly, he wrapped the belt around the scabbard, drew his arm back and flung the sword. It arced high, flipping end over end, and descended towards the water. We held our breath, waiting for it to splash into the lake and disappear forever. But, as it neared the surface, a hand came up from below, reaching high, the slender arm draped in shimmering silk. The hand grabbed the sword and, holding it straight up, pointing at the gloomy sky, slowly disappeared beneath the surface. When the tip of the scabbard was gone, the lake returned to how it had been—smooth as glass, without a single ripple.

I let out a breath. "Did you see that?"

Bedivere nodded. "The legends are true. By the gods, I admit I had my doubts." He looked around, his eyes wide, as if he had just come to his senses. "I have squandered precious time," he said. "Quickly. We must return to Arthur,"

Chapter 23

Mitch

We rode for nearly an hour, fast for the first half hour, and then, when the land turned from grassy plains to brush and trees, we slowed to a canter, then a trot. The cart was well behind us, long out of sight, but still Merlin pressed us forward. When the ground turned soft, we walked the horses, and then left them tethered in a clearing and continued on foot. The land was damp, and my feet sank into the earth as I walked through the waist-high grass. We weren't in a swamp, but it only needed a sharp rain shower to become one. I wondered how, or if, the cart would make it through.

Ahead of us, not far away, a large hill rose from the flat land. We made for that, and soon I saw it wasn't rising from the ground, but a lake. The closer we got, the wetter the land became, and I found myself jumping from one grass tuffet to another and skirting around stagnant pools. The others weren't having any better time of it. Pendragon carried the sack Aisley had taken from her horse, and held her by an arm to keep her from slipping. They seemed as unfamiliar with this type of landscape as I was. All except Merlin, of course. He walked as if he was on a golf course, the smooth, mowed part, not the rough. Then the ground suddenly became firmer. It looked the same, but our feet no longer sank into the muck. We all stopped, surprised. When I looked, it was possible to see a slight difference in the grass, a lighter strip of green heading straight towards the lake but veering away from the course we had been on.

"The causeway," Merlin said. "From ancient times. One of the secret ways to Avalon."

We followed him, walking single file along the causeway, moving faster now, and soon we were at the edge of the water. It covered everything for miles, it seemed, and wasn't a lake, as such. It was simply a sheet of water that didn't end. Towards the east, it merged into the landscape, going from open water, to marsh, to grassland, and to the west, it grew wider, disappearing into the mist. And from the grey, shimmering sheet, the hill rose, tall and dark and ominous, and slightly familiar, and I recognized it as the mountain in the lake the Talisman had shown me.

"The Isle of Avalon," Merlin said.

"That's the Sacred Tor," I said.

"A tor, yes," Merlin said, "and the sacred temple is within, but the mound is the Isle of Avalon."

I looked again. "It wasn't an island when you brought us here last time," I said. "There was no lake, just a swamp. And we travelled along a secret causeway then, just as we did now."

Merlin's brow furrowed. "I saw you last twenty summers ago, when you gave the Talisman to Arthur."

"That was years ago" I said, thinking of time in my own terms. "We saw the tor when we visited Pendragon's descendant, and we last saw you …"

When? A year ago? Or over a thousand years in the future? I looked back at Merlin, who seemed alarmed.

"You must speak no more of this."

I thought of how the world was on our last visit, and the state that Merlin was in. "But—"

"No," he said, pounding his staff on the ground for emphasis. "I am not a traveller like you. You have seen things I have not, and to tell me the future could change the course of history. Speak no more."

I kept quiet, but the silence soon became awkward, so I asked, "How are we going to get to the tor?"

Merlin, who was now standing with his back to me, staring across the water, said without turning, "There is a boat, hidden among the reeds, not far from here."

"How—"

"Pendragon," Merlin said. "Come. We will need it shortly."

And they left me there with Aisley. I think Merlin needed to process what I'd said. His discomfort worried me. He was always the one in control, who knew what was going to happen, who saved us and helped us, but suddenly he seemed unsure of himself.

Aisley came and stood by my side. "Did you really meet a descendant of my son?" She looked across the water. "Does he visit this place with you?"

I felt myself become more worried. "I don't think I'm supposed to say anything about that."

She kept staring across the lake; I could tell she was disappointed.

"But I don't think it would hurt to tell you that,

yeah, we met some of your descendants." I kept my voice low. Pendragon and Merlin were not far away, thrashing through the reeds, and I didn't want them to hear. "Charlie and I, we met several, but our visits don't happen for a long time. Some, for a very long time."

"You do return, though," Aisley said. "You have visited us once, long ago. Now you return, and you will return again?"

"Yes," I said, "yes, we will."

I thought about telling her that we were, in fact, related, but then I heard gentle splashing on the water and a boat came around the reeds, with Merlin in the bow and Pendragon rowing. They beached the boat where we were standing, and Aisley and I helped pull it onto the shore.

"What now?" I asked.

Merlin sat on the edge of the boat, his staff lying across his lap. "Now we wait," he said, "and hope."

Chapter 24

Charlie

The cart rattled at a good pace over solid ground, but when it became boggy, me and Bedivere had to push from behind while Ennora drove and the horse strained and stumbled in front. The light was starting to dim, and I felt a rising panic that we'd be caught out in the swamp in the dark, and that whatever we were trying to accomplish would slip away from us, like the cloak had slipped away from me.

I was sure I didn't have the strength to push the cart over another tussock when we found ourselves on firm ground. Ennora pulled the horse to a stop.

"It's a path of some sort," Bedivere said. Then he pointed. "And look there, a trail through the grass. Others have come this way, and not long before us."

Bedivere led the horse and I pushed from behind, and Ennora made sure Arthur was comfortable and kept clutching the Talisman, and soon we found the others, waiting by the side of a lake with a big hill sticking up from the middle of it.

"That's the Sacred Tor," I said.

Merlin gave me a strange look, and Mitch came up beside me. "I think he'd rather we didn't talk about that," he said. "Or any of our adventures, unless they took place in the past."

"But they all took place in the past. We saw the tor four years ago."

"Not our past, his past. We visited the Sacred Tor several hundred years in his future."

I rubbed my temples. "This is too confusing."

"Just don't talk about anything, okay? He thinks it's really important."

"What about last time? He needs to know. The Talisman is gone, and looking for it has driven him mad. Don't you think he'd want to know that?"

Merlin came to the cart. "Leave your talking," he said. "We have much to do and little time."

We slid the plank with Arthur lying on it out of the cart and carried it to the boat. It just about fit, and everyone else crowded around it. I helped Bedivere unhitched the cart. I took my sword out and put it in the boat while he tethered the horse. Then we pushed the boat off the shore, and I clambered in, squeezing between Mitch and Ennora.

Bedivere took the oars and manoeuvred us into the open water. Pendragon sat in the stern and Merlin sat in the bow, gazing at the tor, and giving an occasional order to Bedivere to veer left or right. We sat in silence, gliding over the water, as evening mists began to swirl around the lake. I watched the tor loom closer. It rose steeply from the water, vibrant green against the slate sky, lined with shrubs that grew on the edges of the cuttings made in the hillside. I knew they formed a path, a maze that led from the main opening to the top of the tor. The path ran round and round the tor, climbing higher with each circuit so that, from a distance, the tor looked striped.

The crossing was short. Bedivere and Merlin manoeuvred the boat to a relatively flat piece of ground and, as soon as we touched land, Pendragon jumped out and pulled the boat up the shore while we all scrambled out of it. At Merlin's insistence, we pulled the boat fully out of the water and onto the side of the hill, with Arthur lying in it, covered with his cloak, as if he was in an open coffin.

We gathered around, looking, not at Arthur, but Merlin. We had brought Arthur to the Isle of Avalon, but none of us knew what to do next. Then Merlin, standing near the bow of the boat and looking across the lake, began to speak.

"Within this tor, a temple waits. A temple that joins the heavens and the Land. The Talisman must now take its place in that temple. A Guardian must open the door, and a Guardian's hand—a hand that Arthur's blood flows through—must join the Talisman with the Sacred Temple. The Prophecy tells us that he who is the living King when that union occurs shall be the Eternal King, and he will watch over the Land, and he and his knights will rise to defend the Land when it is in peril."

Merlin stepped to the side of the boat and gently pulled the cloak off Arthur, being careful not to jar the Talisman out of his hands. He laid it over one arm, then bent and picked up my sword in his free hand.

"The Guardians will come with me," he said. "Bedivere, stay with your King." He turned to Aisley and Ennora. "Comfort him. Do not let his spirit flag."

He handed my sword to me. "This you will need.

Your task is to get us to the temple as quickly as possible." Then he turned to Mitch and gave him the cloak. "It is your task to get us inside the tor, into the Sacred Temple, for only a Guardian, wearing Arthur's cloak, can open the door." Mitch nodded, looking doubtful.

Pendragon stepped forward. "What is my task?"

"The most important of all. You will take the Talisman."

Pendragon shook his head. "Should not that honour go to Mitch or Charlie, who have travelled the ages?"

"We all have our part to play," Merlin said. "They will play theirs in time."

"But am I worthy? The issue of Arthur's daughter, from a union with a fruit seller?"

Merlin looked across the lake, at the gathering gloom and thickening mist.

"Why would you hold a woman's bloodline less potent than a man's. If anything, it is stronger. It is the woman who gives the man life, and to whom he clings, on whom he depends."

Merlin went back to the boat and looked down at Arthur. "Now comes the most dangerous part of this quest." Arthur's eyes were closed, his breathing shallow. "We must take the Talisman from him. It is all that is keeping him alive. The journey to the temple is short, but like the short journey from the mother's womb into the world, it can too easily end in tragedy. If the Talisman is not joined with the temple while Arthur is alive, then all is for naught, and the Land will die with him."

He bent low. "Sire," he said, his voice soft, "it is time."

Arthur opened his eyes. "Is it over?"

"Not yet, but soon."

"I feel stronger," Arthur said, "rested."

"That, I fear, will pass. The Talisman must be taken to the temple. It can no longer protect you. But you must hold on until the task is complete."

"The Prophecy?"

"Depends on you, and your strength."

He motioned for Pendragon to come forward. Arthur looked up at him. "Grandson. How I wish I could have taken you into my court to serve as one of my Knights of the Table."

Pendragon laid a hand on Arthur's chest. "It was enough to have served you these few hours."

"Charlie," Merlin called. "Straight up the side of the Tor. Five levels. Cut a path for us to follow and wait for us. Quick as you can."

Then he turned back to Pendragon. "Take the Talisman, and follow."

Pendragon eased the black stone from Arthur's hands. Arthur sank into his pillows, his face grey. "Stay with him," Merlin said to Bedivere, Aisley, and Ennora. "Keep him alive."

He turned abruptly, heading for the tor, "Follow," he said. "Quickly."

I scrambled up the steep bank, swinging my sword at the first barrier of bushes.

Chapter 25

Mitch

We headed up the side of the tor, climbing quickly, with Merlin and Charlie in the lead, followed by Pendragon, and then me. Merlin pointed the way, and Charlie hacked the shrubs guarding the paths. It was a difficult climb, but going up the side was still faster than following the meandering path.

Charlie hacked, then slipped through to the next level. Merlin followed. Then Pendragon. The hill was steep, and clawing my way up with one hand while holding Arthur's cloak in the other was awkward and slow. Soon, Pendragon and the others were well ahead, leaving me scrambling to catch up. It was exhausting, and I began to panic, worrying that we would fail because I couldn't keep up.

I dropped the cloak and wasted precious seconds putting it on. It dragged behind me and caught on the shrubs, but having both hands free meant I could climb faster. After two more levels, I caught sight of Pendragon. I climbed faster, my legs and lungs burning. One level above, Charlie swung his sword, slicing through branches, hacking at the trunks. A sliver of darkening sky showed through the green, and he disappeared through it.

I pulled myself up the bank as quickly as I could,

squirmed through the gap, and onto the pathway. We were nearly halfway up the tor and I wondered if I had the strength to finish the climb. Then I saw that the others had not continued up the slope. Charlie was sitting on the ground, gasping for breath, his sword lying at his feet. Pendragon stood nearby, watching Merlin, who was looking at a large rock.

It was white, like chalk, and shaped like a giant egg. It also looked out of place, for I had seen no other rocks anywhere near that size or shape on the island. It gave me a jolt of deja vu, but that was chased away when Merlin turned to me. "This way," he said, motioning to the rock. "Quickly."

I crossed the path and stood in front of the stone.

"The entrance to the temple is here," Merlin said, "sealed when the work was completed. You must open the portal."

"How am I supposed to do that?" I asked.

"Turn the stone."

"Huh?"

I felt like I'd been punched in the gut. This was where it was all going to fall apart, and it would be my fault. I suddenly felt very alone.

Charlie picked up his sword and stood beside me. "It's not like a doorknob. You'll need to grip it somehow."

I looked at the rock. It was smooth, but that wasn't the problem. The problem was, it was huge, and probably very heavy. "It's not a question of gripping it," I said, "it's a question of turning it. It's simply not possible."

"This Isle of Avalon is a mystic place," Merlin

said, "a curtain between our world and the world of the spirits. It holds great powers, powers honed to prepare for the Eternal King. The temple below awaits Arthur, and its power makes all things possible. You are a Guardian, you wear the cloak of Arthur Pendragon, King of the Britons, the temple will open for you. Place your hands on the stone, believe, and turn it."

I placed my palms against the stone. It was cold, and felt as solid as the hill itself. It couldn't turn, but I couldn't think that way. I put my hands on either side of the rock and tried to turn it like a steering wheel. Nothing happened. I might as well have been trying to turn the Tor itself. I felt Merlin's eyes on me, and Charlie by my side, willing it to work. My stomach knotted, knowing I was going to have to tell them I failed.

Then I remembered why this all looked familiar. This was the place Malcolm had led us to. The pathways had been here, but the shrub barriers were gone. We had chased Falan and Lubbock to this place. But there was a door in the hillside then, with steps leading down. And Lubbock's body at the bottom. I remembered the passageway, and the temple, a great cathedral, with columns and an altar and a crushing sense of sadness. And Falan waiting.

I pushed those thoughts away. That was a tragedy looming in the future, that we had lived through years ago. The only thing that mattered was, it had happened. If these dreams, these adventures, truly were real, then we had been in the temple already. Or we would be in a few hundred years. Either way, what it proved was, the doorway did exist, and it could be opened. And the stone, it hadn't been as prominent, barring part of the path. It hadn't been turned over; it had been swivelled to rest against the side of the tor.

I drew a calming breath, placed my hand against the cool, hard stone, and pushed. It turned easily. I jumped back, surprised.

A low rumble began, like a small earthquake. Then it grew louder. The hillside shook and a split appeared a few feet from the rock. The split turned into a gap, running about ten feet up from the edge of the path. The gap widened, sending stones and dirt cascading onto the path. When it was about three feet wide, it stopped.

The door, the portal, the opening, it was there before us, and the stone steps were there too, leading into the darkness below.

We all stared in wonder, but Merlin didn't waste time gaping. He rushed through the opening, shouting for us to follow.

We ran down the steps after him, the light growing dimmer as we descended. At the bottom of the stairs, we entered a wide hallway. The fading daylight from above was gone, yet we could still see, and I remembered from our previous visit that the underground chambers glowed. Not a lot, just enough to see grey outlines of each other, and the dimensions of the cavern. I took a quick look for Lubbock's skeleton, but realized it wouldn't be there for a few more centuries. We ran after Merlin, following the hallway and his echoing footsteps.

We ran on a downward slope, deep into the tor, where the air was dank and moist and cold. A feeling of expectation overcame me. I remembered the sadness from our last visit, but there was none of that now, just a neutral feeling. One of waiting.

Suddenly, the hallway ended. We all stopped. Merlin stood in front of us, in a large room, so large, we couldn't see the walls or ceiling. Widely spaced columns gave a sense of the scale, but that was all we could see. That, and the altar, glowing with soft, white light against the far wall.

Chapter 26

Charlie

I came to a halt behind Merlin. Then Pendragon bumped into my back. The room was huge, with massive columns rising into the blackness. I remembered it being lit with an eerie green light, and feeling as if my heart was going to break. But none of that was here now, just the columns, and the altar.

It was intricately carved into the rock face that formed the far wall, depicting a raised platform, a table and a cross, a bulky thing adorned with knots and intertwining ropes. At its centre was a black circle, a hole, just big enough for the Talisman.

I felt an overwhelming awe, and it suddenly occurred to me that I was the only one wearing a sword. The place was sacred, and being armed felt out of place. I took the sword off and leaned it against the nearest column. Then I stepped forward, along with Mitch and Pendragon, until we were standing next to Merlin.

"The sacred cross," he said, pointing towards the altar, "the receptacle, the resting place of the Talisman."

He turned to Pendragon. "Go, now, before it is too late."

"What do I do?"

"Place the Talisman into the centre of the cross. Hurry. For your grandfather's sake."

Pendragon didn't hesitate. He ran across the stone floor and climbed onto the platform, then stretched out his hand holding the Talisman. The cross, with its receptacle, was too far away. He pulled himself up, using patterns in the carving of the table as foot and hand holds. He stretched out again. The Talisman hovered over the hole. He pressed it in. A sharp click echoed through the vast room as it settled into position.

Pendragon jumped down and ran back to Merlin.

And nothing happened.

For a few horrible moments I thought we had been too late. Arthur had died and there was no king to make eternal. But then the altar, already the brightest thing in the room, began to glow, sending streaks of light into the gloom. Then the room itself, the floor, the walls, the ceiling, glowed white, bathing everything in such stark light it became hard to see.

A rumble, louder than the one we had heard when the portal opened, came from beneath the floor. I felt my legs vibrating. Then the rumble became a roar, as a jagged crack shot across the floor from wall to wall, about three feet in front of the altar.

"It's starting," Merlin shouted, his voice edged with glee. "Move back, against the wall."

We moved back as the crack widened. From below came a roar and flickering, yellow light. Then flames shot out of the crevasse, reaching high into the air. I should have been scared, but I felt calm, happy, and, as I realized this was the second flame the Talisman had shown me, I also understood that the first was the burning of our cloak. This brought a sense of peace. The Talisman had predicted this. It was meant to be, and we were where we belonged. Fighting it was no use.

Then, through the ceiling of the cathedral, which we could now see far above us, tendrils of what looked like smoke appeared. But they weren't made of smoke, because they were drifting down, through the rock ceiling, into the chamber. There were ten or more, then fifty, then hundreds, thousands, all individual trails of white mist, floating into the flaming chasm.

"The spirits of Arthur's knights," Merlin said, shouting to be heard above the roar. "They will rest here, and watch, and wait."

Such a feeling of joy spread through me that I began to laugh. Then Mitch laughed, and Pendragon. We watched the spirits, and felt their joy, and wiped tears of laughter from our eyes. It was such a release. The first time in days—since we had arrived, in fact— that we were in no danger. Even the idea of spending the rest of my life in the Dark Ages didn't dent my happiness.

"They will sleep here," Merlin continued, "held safe until they are called to defend the Land. If such a time comes, if the Land is in peril, and the Talisman remains in place, they will rise to fight once more."

Soon, the cascade of spirits thinned and stopped. The chasm roared, the ground shook and rumbled, the gap closed, and the crack disappeared, leaving us bathed in the white light that now glowed from every surface.

"All is well," Merlin said.

We stopped laughing, but the feeling of joy remained. Merlin, himself, smiled as he turned to us and said, "We must now hasten to Arthur's side."

We went back through the hall at a trot, up the slope to the base of the stairs. Outside, the light had dimmed.

"Mitch," Merlin said, "close the entrance."

Without a word, Mitch, still wearing Arthur's cloak, went to the strange stone and turned it back to the way it had been. The gap rumbled and closed, and soon it was impossible to see it had been there. It was then I realized I had forgotten my sword. I was going to say something, but I didn't feel like I would need it.

Going down the hill was a lot easier than climbing up. We slid down the slopes and squeezed through the gaps I had made, and soon we were at the shore where Bedivere, Aisley and Ennora clustered around the boat. They turned towards us, silent, with faces that conveyed concern. My stomach dropped. Had we been too late, after all?

Arthur was in the boat, where we had left him, on the plank that had carried him from the battle. But he no longer looked frail and weak. The bandage on his head was gone, as was the wound, and his hair—now red and flowing to his shoulders—was no longer matted with blood. His clothes were clean and free from rips and cuts. In fact, they weren't his clothes at all. He was now wearing a white shroud that reached to his feet, and he lay with his hands folded over his chest, resting on the symbol of a red dragon. His skin, white and smooth as marble, made him look like a statue of himself as a young man.

"He glowed," Bedivere said. "He was slipping

away, and then light formed around him, so bright we had to step away. And now ..."

"Is he dead?" Aisley asked.

Merlin placed a hand on Arthur's forehead. "No, he sleeps. Arthur is safe now, ready for his journey."

"Journey?" I asked, not sure I was ready for another trek.

But Merlin said nothing. He turned to the lake, looking into the mist. We all followed his gaze, and, in moments, we saw it—a low, flat boat coming out of the mist, with four shrouded figures on it. As they neared, I could see they were women, all in white, with veils over their faces and dressed in the delicate, white material I had seen on the arm coming out of the lake. In the centre of the boat, about two feet high, was a raised platform, covered in large, white pillows. Each of the four women stood at one of its corners.

The boat drew near, as if guided by an unseen hand, and stopped when it touched the shore.

The women said nothing. They simply looked at Merlin, who nodded to them and then to us.

Bedivere and Pendragon took one end of the board and me and Mitch the other. We lifted Arthur and walked slowly, carrying him to the boat. We struggled a little, for the bank was steep and climbing onto the boat was awkward, but no one—Merlin, the women, or Aisley and Ennora—said a word. Once on the boat we set the plank on the deck and Bedivere and Pendragon lifted Arthur and laid him on the pillows.

We left the boat as we had come, awkwardly and

without a word. Once we were back on land, the women looked again at Merlin, who nodded in return.

That was the only communication with them. They silently turned towards Arthur looking down on him as the boat slipped away, returning to the mist, leaving not a ripple behind.

Chapter 27

Mitch

"It's over," Merlin said.

I reflected for a moment, on the battle, the destruction, the hideous loss of life. It had not ended well, but it had ended, and that was good enough.

Evening drew in, the mists that the barge had disappeared into thickened. We huddled together for warmth, wondering what to do next. There was no question of trying to leave the island, not with the darkness coming and the fog too thick to see through. We'd end up going in circles. And, for me and Charlie, there remained the question of what to do about our knowledge of the future of the Talisman.

The Land was safe, Merlin had told us, as long as the Talisman remained in its receptacle. And we knew it didn't. We knew it became lost. And I knew that the loss of it had driven Merlin insane. If the Talisman, and the Sacred Temple, and the Isle of Avalon were so important for the safety of the Land, then he needed to know.

"We should gather wood," Bedivere said, "and light a fire." He didn't sound hopeful. There wasn't much on the island outside of the shrubs used as boarders for the paths, and I doubted that anyone had brought a box of matches with them. But Aisley and

Ennora went off, searching the edges of the island, gathering what sticks they could find.

Bedivere had no sword, but he did have a knife, which he used to shave bits of wood off the board we had carried Arthur on. With the shavings, and the wood the women gathered, and the flint and steel Merlin produced from the bag on his belt, they soon had a fire going.

"There are blankets and pillows in the boat," Bedivere said. "We can make ourselves comfortable with them until dawn."

I realized I was still wearing Arthur's cloak. I took it off and held it in front of me. It was bloody and torn from battle, and muddy where I had trailed it down the bank towards the boat, but it would still be a good substitute for a blanket. "You can use this too," I said. But Merlin shook his head.

"The cloak has other plans."

Everyone seemed to be doing something. Aisley and Ennora had returned to their task of scrounging up firewood, and Charlie was helping Pendragon and Bedivere get anything useful out of the boat. I was as alone with Merlin as I was ever going to be, and I didn't know what the next day would bring. So, I thought I should try again.

"Merlin," I said. "What we did today, what happened with the Talisman, you need to know—"

I was afraid he'd get mad at me, like the last time, but his face remained soft, and all he did was raise his hand. "We will talk," he said, "but not here."

He turned away. Aisley and Ennora came back with another small bundle of sticks. They and

Pendragon built up the fire, and Bedivere turned the boat on its side to use as a shelter, spreading the blankets and pillows next to it.

"You will spend the night here," Merlin pronounced, as if he was telling them something they didn't know. Then he continued. "Charlie, Mitch, and I will climb to the top of the mount. In the morning, we will travel back to Arthur's camp."

Aisley came to us, holding the sack she'd had tied to her saddle. "If you are to spend the night on the summit, you'll need these to keep warm." She handed the sack to Charlie. Then Ennora came to us, and they embraced us in a group hug.

"Thank you," Aisley said, "for bringing my son back to me."

"And my husband," Ennora said.

"I'm not sure we did much—"

"You do yourself a disservice," Ennora said. "You are brave knights, and I will tell my daughters and daughters-in-law your story. The women of our family will keep your story alive, and they will wait for your return. The return of the brave knights of long ago, who come to save the Land."

We said good night to Bedivere and Pendragon, who embraced me so hard I thought he might crack my ribs.

"You fought well. Arthur could have asked for no braver knights. And you saved my family. I am in your debt."

I didn't bother pointing out that Aisley had saved my life, and that if anyone carried a debt, it was me. I just thanked him for all he had done, and then we prepared to leave.

Merlin took no blankets. All we had was the cloak, which I folded into a bundle I could carry easily, and whatever was in the sack that Aisley gave us, which Charlie now had.

We left them and went up the trail we had made, scrambling up the steep hill after Merlin. We weren't racing against time, like we were on our first trip, but darkness was falling, so we made as much haste as we could, and it didn't take long to reach the path where the entrance to the Sacred Temple was. From there, we followed the pathway that wound around the tor, walking quickly behind Merlin as he led the way. The path was flat and the incline gentle, so we made good time, but the trail meandered, and by the time we arrived at the summit, it was nearly dark.

At the top, having left the pathway and the shrubs that boarded it behind, we saw the land spreading out in all directions. In the west, the sun had set, though the clouds still glowed, bathing the land in golden light. Below, the sheet of water remained shrouded in mist, and the distant land disappeared into darkness. To the east, a range of faraway hills stood, barely visible against the dark sky.

The top of the tor was long and narrow and covered in tall grass. With no protection, the wind became stronger and brought with it a sharp chill. We followed Merlin, who led us across the open summit, to a stone at the far end. It was roughly cut into a square and standing on end, reaching about ten feet into the air. Merlin ran his hand over its surface.

"The obelisk ," he said. "Sit here, on this side, out of the wind. This is where we talk."

Chapter 28

Charlie

I wasn't sure what he wanted to talk about, but I was glad to get out of the wind. We sat on the ground at the base of the pillar, facing east, where a line of distant hills was still visible against the darkening sky. For a while, we sat in silence, resting and watching the night draw in. Then Merlin pointed towards the horizon.

"Look there," he said. "What do you see."

I looked, seeing nothing but the hills. And in a few minutes, I wouldn't even be able to see them.

"I see hills," I said.

Mitch nodded. "Yeah, that's about it."

Merlin sighed, but it wasn't from weariness or woe. It was a sigh of contentment.

"I am not a traveller as you are. And I therefore do not see time as you do. You have seen days that are yet ahead of me, times when we shall meet again. You know of events that, in your life, have already happened, but which a mere wizard cannot know."

He lowered his hand, but I kept my eyes on the darkening hills.

"I see time as that range of hills," he said. "There are peaks and valleys, light and dark, and those that are behind me I see clearly. But look further, and the hills fade to mist. They are there, I can see them, but only as shadows. And those shadows must not be disturbed."

He leaned back against the stone.

"What do we do with all this knowledge, then?" Mitch asked.

"Keep it inside you," Merlin said, "as I did on our first meeting."

He went silent after that, and I wondered what he was getting at. Then I understood.

"When we first met you," I said, "it wasn't the first time you had met us. We'd been with you hundreds of years earlier, with the Romans, and Kayla."

Merlin nodded. "And had I told you what was in store for you, would you have returned?"

The night was now truly upon us. I shivered in the dark, looking at the black horizon where hardly a hill remained visible. "Yeah," I said, "I get it."

I heard Mitch shift as he wrapped his arms around himself for warmth. "Me too."

"So, we're going to have to keep the secret for the rest of our lives? What if we slip up, or you weaken and come to us, begging for a peek into the future? What then?"

"And beyond that," Mitch said, "what's going to happen to us?"

"Happen?" Merlin asked.

"Yeah," I said. "Our cloak is gone. We're stuck here now. What are we supposed to do, and how are we supposed to keep quiet about everything we've done?"

Merlin chuckled. "You do not know the power of the Isle of Avalon."

"But our cloak," I said.

"Your cloak was imbued with such power because it belonged to Arthur." He took Arthur's cloak from Mitch and, rising to his feet, unfolded it and held it up. "This is now your cloak, and this will bring you home."

Mitch ran his hand over the scarred material. "All we need to do, then, is travel back to Horsham?"

Merlin draped the cloak over our shoulders. We sat close, pulling it around us, grateful for what little warmth it provided. "You appear in Horsham, at a sacred place, where the wall between the worlds is thin. But you now sit atop the largest conduit from this world to the others. This cloak, and the power of the Tor will take you home."

"Are you saying that we can go home? From here? Right now?" As soon as I asked, I was sorry, fearing the hope rising in my chest like an over-inflated balloon would pop. But Merlin simply smiled.

"Of course," he said. "But first, open the sack."

I looked down at the sack I had been carrying, the one Aisley had brought with her from Sussex, the one she had almost died rescuing from her horse as Mordred's army crashed down on us. I pulled at the knot and looked inside.

"Our clothes," I said. "Our real clothes."

Despite their journey, they were clean, neatly folded, and smelled of soap.

We quickly changed, not only because we wanted

to go home, but because we were freezing. When we finished, Merlin told us to lay down at the base of the pillar.

"Farewell," he said, covering us with Arthur's cloak, "until we meet again."

We lay side by side, in the same position as when we had arrived. Above us, unseen, Merlin waited.

I thought about him meeting us again. That would be in his future, several hundred years from the time we were in now. And he would meet us again, and again, always there to help us with his strength and knowledge, always striving to save the Talisman, until its loss became too much for him. I wondered, if in our future, we would ever see him again, and I decided, despite how sad it made me, that we would not.

And then I fell asleep.

Chapter 29
Tuesday, 16 June 2019

Mitch

In my dream, I was falling. It wasn't alarming, it was more like I was floating, drifting forward through the years, past the troubles and turmoil we had seen, to the safe, suburban home where our parents waited.

Oh, yeah, our parents.

Panic shook the dream. I landed on my bed and woke up.

I pushed the cloak off. Charlie opened his eyes, and we sat up. Mom and Dad were both there, standing over us. Behind them the door was open, and a splintered chair lay in front of it. Dad was breathing hard, but mom was hardly breathing. Their eyes were wide and white.

"What … you … you," Dad said.

"The swords," Mom said.

"We lost them," Charlie said.

"But … you disappeared," Dad said, his voice quiet and dreamy, "you seemed to just … you were there … then you weren't. And now you're back."

"Where did you go?" Mom asked.

"It doesn't really matter," I said. I gathered up the cloak and held it out to her. Thankfully, the blood

173

and mud hadn't travelled back with us, but the cloak was still ripped and frayed. "Take this, do what you want with it. Burn it, cut it up, throw it in the trash."

She took it from my hands, slowly drawing it into her arms and hugging it against her chest. "Are you sure?"

"Sure," Charlie said.

"But," Dad sputtered, "you ran. You locked your door. And you need—"

Mom put a hand on his arm. "It's all right, dear. I don't think they need a punishment."

She turned him, and led him towards the door, talking in soothing tones.

"We don't have to worry about this anymore. We can put it behind us. We don't need to think about it."

Then she turned and looked at us, her expression a mixture of sadness and relief.

"It's over."

Author's Note

When I first began writing *The Sacred Tor*, I knew I needed something for the Talisman to do. I decided on the Glastonbury Tor as a location, and an underground temple as the venue. I also needed a way to get into the underground temple, and my solution to that was a big rock, something easily recognizable that would stay in the same place for centuries.

The entrance, I decided, would be on the south side of the tor, on the fifth level—mainly to keep my protagonists from needing to climb to the top—and the big rock would act as a key.

All these were the sorts of spur-of-the-moment decisions writers make all the time. And then have to live with.

The tor, along with the underground temple, appears in three of the books. When I was writing the final book, I needed some additional local colour, so I fired up Google Earth and had a close look at the Glastonbury Tor. This was the first time I saw, or even heard of, the Egg Stone.

The Glastonbury Tor Egg Stone, or Dragon's Egg, is nestled against the south side of the tor, on the fifth level. Legends tell of it being the marker to the entrance of an underground labyrinth. It was so near to what I had imagined it was spooky.

In the first editions of *The Sacred Tor* and *The Isle of*

Avalon, the stone, as I imagined it, was visible in the tor's side, like a big, moon-like circle of rock. After encountering the Dragon's Egg, both on the web and in real life, (having discovered it on Google, I travelled to the Glastonbury Tor to see it myself) I changed the final book, *The Talisman*, to reflect how the Egg actually sits on the ground, and modified the others in the rewrite.

That minor detail does not detract from the fact that I imagined the Egg Stone, its location, and purpose, before I even knew it existed.

Things like that make writing exciting and worthwhile, as well as making books-in-progress seem like they were meant to be.

Author's photo of The Dragon's Egg,
Glastonbury Tor, south side, fifth level.

About the Author

Michael Harling is originally from upstate New York. He moved to Britain in 2002 and currently lives in Sussex.

Lindenwald Press
Sussex, United Kingdom

Printed in Great Britain
by Amazon